Separate Lives

Separate Lives

QUINN SMITH

SEPARATE LIVES

This is a work of fiction. All of the characters, names, incidents, organizations, and dialogue in this novel are either the products of the author's imagination or are used fictitiously.

iUniverse books may be ordered through booksellers or by contacting:

iUniverse
1663 Liberty Drive
Bloomington, IN 47403
www.iuniverse.com
1-800-Authors (1-800-288-4677)

ISBN: 978-1-6632-0359-5 (sc)
ISBN: 978-1-6632-0360-1 (e)

Library of Congress Control Number: 2020911286

Print information available on the last page.

iUniverse rev. date: 06/27/2020

Dedication

This book is dedicated to my family, church members, sorority sisters and friends. Thanks for pushing me along to finish this project by asking, "How's the book coming," or "Did you finish that book, yet" or "Are you done - I can't wait to read your book." Your sincere reminders that I could do it, were heart-warming.

To my husband, Julian, my children: Anastasia, Julian II. and Regina; you are my biggest cheerleaders and I appreciate your support. Mommy loves you! My sisters: Shaweda, Susan and Sherrye were very encouraging and provided many needed diversions. I'm ready to plan our next trip – plane, train, boat or automobile?

To my sorority sisters of Zeta Phi Beta Sorority, Incorporated – The Astounding Alpha Eta Zeta Chapter (Memphis), I love y'all sooo much – thanks for the Sisterly Love and inspiration!

Last, but certainly not least, I want to thank my number #1 fan, my mother, Doris Regina Quinn for pouring into me all her gifts. She is me and I am her. She has truly been the wind beneath my wings, and I am profoundly grateful for her guidance and love.

You may see yourselves in some of this story, but do not get excited, the names were changed to protect the innocent.

Enjoy the read!

Stacey Jill (Quinn) Smith

Note: If there are any similarities to anybody you know or any places you have been, it is purely coincidental; this book is fiction.

Chapter 1

Gail wanted her old yearbooks, her art portfolio, her cat figurine collection, and her cassette tapes from her mother's house. As she drove down I55 North interstate in her royal blue SAAB Sedan from New Orleans, Louisiana headed to Memphis, Tennessee, she realized she would have to find a cassette player to play the cassettes. Thinking out loud, she said, "I had some jamming music." She selected Janet Jackson's *Control* album from her play list and started bopping her head to her mantra for the 80s. She sang out loud for a few miles to, *What Have You Done for Me Lately, When I Think of You, Control, The Pleasure Principle and Nasty* and then decided to slow it down when she saw the sign for Little Rock, Arkansas with Raphael Saadiq's, *All Hits at The House of Blues*. When she was 20 miles away from home, she changed from satellite radio and tuned into the local gospel station; she did not want to arrive at her mother's house jamming & booming her car stereo system. The gospel station, *Praises*, was a station she could enjoy in New Orleans; they played old and new gospel music. They also broadcasted church services, entertainment news, and human-interest stories, so sometimes she would get some insights into what was going on in Memphis. One of her high school classmates was the lead disc jockey, so he would oftentimes refer to their school. He would say, "Those Cougars are at it again, doing great things in the city," when doing a special news feature and it just happened to spotlight an alumnus. He would add, "I knew she was smart and would end up doing something." He was funny in high school; Gail knew he would end up doing something in television or radio. He was a junior when she was a senior, but she got to know him by working on the yearbook staff.

Gail kept the old yearbooks from middle school and high school because they were the ones she helped edit and she loved seeing her name in print. Even though some of her classmates later claimed they only saw her on almost every page, she really thought she did a good job in showing the diversity of the schools and having a variety of students in the candid shots. Her Advisors should have pointed out any disparities; she had a good time getting to know her classmates and working with a staff. She got to go to all events free and she was able to leave class early to interview students, staff, or special guests. Editing the yearbooks helped with her writing, communication, and social skills.

She strongly considered majoring in Art in college because she loved drawing, painting, and sculpting. Her high school Guidance Counselor, Ms. Pugh, encouraged her to major in her strongest skillset, English. Ms. Pugh had a way of convincing you that you could do anything and be anything with the right guidance. Her high school art teacher, Ms. Steinbridge, said Gail had a good eye for art and was a great talent in art. When they went to visit museums on field trips, Gail would gravitate to Vincent Van Gogh-like work; he was her favorite artist. When she heard his story and Ms. Steinbridge showed the movie, *Lust for Life* starring Kirk Douglas, she loved Van Gogh even more. Her art portfolio is filled with her attempts to capture Van Gogh's most famous pieces including different versions of sunflowers. She wanted to create a collage of the best ones and hang them in her office.

The cat collection was simply adorable, and she left them at her mother's house because she did not want to risk breaking them in her many travels. There are 26 in all and they have a 3-part glass display case. Some are porcelain, some are jade, some are glass, some are wood, and some are metal. They are brightly colored and light up the room with the cats posing with different expressions in different directions. Even though it was a major expense when she ordered them for what she thought was a onetime price of $9.95. She knew it was too good to be true, but she ordered them, without her mother's permission, anyway. The first 8 cats came in the mail and they were beautiful in the glass display case. Another 4 came, but this time with a bill and then another 4 came with another bill. Before Gail knew it, she had 26 cats, 3 glass cases and a bill for $192.00. It took forever to pay her mother back for covering the cost without it going to a collection agency. She cherishes her cat collection and wants to share it with her children. Even though they do not have any pets, Gail hopes this will give them an appreciation for collectibles.

Gail ordered cassette tapes through a music club she joined from one of the magazines or comic books she and her sisters were always reading. This one-time only order of 10 of your favorite artists also resulted in a huge bill where she ended up having to re-pay her Mom for the over 100 cassettes she ended up with when the music club contract ended. The cassettes featured the most popular music in all genres, so Gail was able to listen to a variety of music. She had pop, country, soul, jazz and classical. What she did not have, which she was starting to enjoy was rap. Nevertheless, she popped a cassette in her cassette player almost every day after school while sitting on the porch while waiting on dinner or when she was outside playing jacks. She carried her pink and blue cassette player around everywhere and had a separate clear case where she stored the cassette tapes. She would play with them on the porch like dolls – lining the cases up, putting genres together, matching male with female singers and pretending to be a disc jockey as she introduced each song before playing it.

Her mother told everybody she was ready to move into an independent living senior facility called, Tara Manor. She was tired of having to pay someone to maintain the yard, paint the house, fix plumbing issues, etc. Since she lived alone, she did not like having strangers come into her house. She was paranoid from watching all the crime shows detailing how seniors were always being taken advantage of in one way or another. She also watched the news religiously and unfortunately a lot of the bad news reported was coming from her area. She also did not like the way her neighbors were handling business across the street. She knew they were selling drugs or something. All she started seeing was police cars riding up and down the street. She simply did not feel comfortable or safe. She did not sleep well at night and was often startled by loud music, roaring cars, and sudden gun shots. Sometimes people would knock on her door late at night and really gave her a fright. She stopped walking to church, she stopped walking to the mailbox, she stopped walking to the corner store, and she stopped sitting on the porch. She left a message on Gail's work voice mail two weeks ago, "Hey baby girl, if you want your old stuff, you better come and get it before I leave, which will be at the end of the month." Gail called her sister; Adrianne to make sure her Mom had not sold the house yet. "We're still packing up stuff; you can come on home and look for your things. I'll leave them in a separate box for you." As the music slowed down and she approached the exit, Gail saw familiar scenery. She began to reminisce and think of her fondest childhood memories; she could only remember as far back as age 11.

April Gail Quincy was an outgoing 11-year old with three sisters and one brother. April preferred to be called Gail, so around the house and in the neighborhood, everybody called her Gail. When she was at school or at church, everybody called her April. She was a caramel-colored little girl with sandy brown short hair and blazing dark brown eyes to match. She wore beige-framed plastic oval-shaped glasses that gave her a futuristic look. She kept her hair in at least 3 ponytails and tried to match everything daily. Her three sisters, Adrianne, Alexandria, Angela and her brother Aldwin made sure she looked her best when she was going to school and to church. She loved to look through the Sears & Roebuck catalog, *Wishbook* and mark items for her "Wish List." She would pick not only toys and clothes, but she would choose household items too. "We need new curtains, I'll order these," she would mumble to herself. Her mother would see her *ordering* things and say, "Don't forget we need some new silverware" or some other obsolete item. Her mother would gladly play along because it kept Gail busy and kept her wishful. Her mother, Jean Marie Quincy, a licensed practical nurse (LPN) at the local hospital worked 7a – 3p and sometimes 3p – 11p. She was a single mother, but she made sure her children had everything they needed to be healthy and happy. April did not quite remember her father, since her mother divorced him when she was five years old. Many said he was tall, dark, and handsome and people often said that her brother, Aldwin looked just like him. April did not think so, because when her father visited them, he was a skinny man with gray hair, false teeth and did not know or remember anybody's names. He never knew who was who and called everybody the wrong name. "Which one are you?" he would say in a serious tone. "I'm Gail," she would chime in like an introduction on a comedy special. Her father would always respond, "Of course you are Gail," and continue to make false promises about coming back to take them to the movies or to the zoo. April did not miss having him around, because she does not remember him. You cannot miss what you never had.

Gail thought about her sisters and how much fun they used to have all by themselves. She particularly remembered one summer when everybody was anxious before her brother was leaving for the military. Her oldest sister, Adrianne, who was 17 years old this particular summer was in charge when their mother was at work or asleep. Adrianne liked to dress like hippies and wore her hair in natural styles; she especially liked wearing afro puffs. When she wore her hair in an afro, she thought she looked like Angela Davis. The big hair was the only similarity. The next sister, Alexandria, who liked to be called Alex, was 15 going on 25. She was the one who always seemed to get in trouble for not being around of for not doing her household chores. "Why aren't these dishes washed," mother would shout when she came home from a late-night shift. Angela would be the one to snitch most of the time. "It was Alex's turn, but she was outside on the porch talking to a boy and didn't do them." Their mother would wake Alex up and make her wash dishes many times that summer. Angela, the 13-year-old sister was the feisty one. You did not want to get on her bad side because she could be very mean. One time she pushed a girl in the dirt while they were playing in the park because she accidentally broke Gail's glasses. She could also be extremely sweet. One summer she brought breakfast to Aldwin in bed for two weeks when he broke his collarbone. Even though her brother, Aldwin was the oldest, he was never home enough to be "in charge." He was always out with his friends playing football or basketball, working at the community center, or hanging out at the house of his girlfriend, Yolandalyn, who he affectionately called, Tootie. Aldwin loved to tease Gail and would often bring her to tears doing so. He would tickle her non-stop or just annoy her with crazy questions. "Why do you have all those barrettes in your hair? What are those earrings matching? Why does your hair always look dirty? Why is your head so big? Why do you play jacks all the time? Why don't you go play in the street? Why do you hold the refrigerator door open so long? Why do you have on socks with sandals?" Since Gail was reflecting, she realized it was harmless fun, but at the time, it really hurt her feelings.

Gail loved attention and she loved to be the center of it. When conversations were not about her, she often tried to shift attention to herself by mentioning something she was doing at school or about something that happened to her outside. Her mother would be the *only* one who appeared to be interested in her story. She would say, "What, wait a minute – everybody, listen to April Gail's story." Gail loved playing outside. Her mother would oftentimes have to call her in when it started to get dark. Gail would make up games for the small children and she would lead the games with kids her own age. She always had to be the leader; she had to oversee giving the rules, the object of the game or the instruction. Everybody relied on her for fun and they knew she would be fair; they waited on her after school and on the weekends. If she did not come outside, they would go to her house to find out where she was and what she was doing.

Gail loved school and the teachers often compared her to her siblings before her. "Oh, you're Angela's little sister, we know you're going to be a good student," some teachers would say. She was a good student, but she soon proved to them that she had her own unique personality and separate aspirations. She was happy that school was just around the corner, because her mother did not have a car, nor did she know how to drive. Gail participated in every extracurricular activity that interested her. She was a cheerleader, edited the newspaper, sang in the Glee Club, worked on the yearbook staff, played tennis, and ran track. Gail's mother was proud that she could do all those extracurricular activities and still be a member of the National Honor Society.

Chapter 2

Gail's reflections, accompanied by some of her favorite music, were interrupted by her cell phone ringing. It was her husband, Garrett, checking on her. "Hey Sweetie, are you there, yet?" he asked. "Almost," Gail answered. "I have about 5 miles to go. I'll call you when I get there." "Okay, love you." Before Gail could respond, he ended the call. Garrett never did like talking on the phone, so he always seemed annoyed when answering the phone. He is not being rude, that is just how he is when it comes to telephone etiquette. Anybody on the other end would think he was mean because he answers the phone very abruptly. Garrett is a Civil Engineer for the city of New Orleans. He enjoys the challenges of his job and prides himself on being able to work remotely on many of the projects. They live in a neighborhood where everyone has been there over 10 years, and everybody knows everybody. That is good and sometimes bad at times. Their Victorian home has a large living room with a fireplace, a huge kitchen with an island, a master bedroom with a balcony, a walk in pantry, a dining room that seats 8, 3 bedrooms, 3 bathrooms, a family room, a bonus room that Gail uses for an office and plenty of space for parties and guests. The grounds are spacious and include a swimming pool, gazebo, fire pit and a water garden. Garrett built a deck around the back area that showcases a small garden; he is very handy and loves to add to the existing architecture. He loves landscaping the yard and is always searching for the perfect bush, tree, or flower to accent the house. "Garrett is always outside doing something," Gail says when someone asks how he is doing. They have three children, Rheanna, age 12, Rochelle, age 10 and Garrett, Jr., age 7. Gail is a curator at one of New Orleans' largest museums. She loves New Orleans because of its nightlife, culture, food, music, art, and history. The museum has a staff of nine and they all have worked there for ten or more years. Gail was fortunate to get the job when Garrett got his job offer 15 years ago. Gail is active in her church, on her job, in her sorority and in her neighborhood.

Gail loves her church and wishes she could be more active. She attends Sunday school regularly, teaches Vacation Bible School in the summer, manages the church website, and helps with the Dance Ministry, but she really wishes she could sing in the church choir. The rehearsal day is never conducive to her work schedule. They generally rehearse on Tuesday nights, which is a big day to unpack and review new inventory. It is also when they have collaboration meetings with other museum staff across the city, so she cannot miss hearing feedback from what others are doing. The only time when she would get to sing was during Women's Month in May. She is an alto and has never led a solo, but she believes she carries a tune well. The Minister of Music is a hard taskmaster who expects nothing less than perfection. The choir has about 75 members with about 40 altos, so they are fine without her. She does not think she would be able to keep up with the demands of choir rehearsal on a regular basis, so it is good that she only participates once a year. If she did join, she would want to give one hundred percent and she knows she would not be able to make the outside engagements, funerals, etc.

Gail has an older staff; there are seven women and two men. She tries to boost their morale by hosting fun events at her house or having professional development sessions at work. She decorates the office for every holiday and brings in treats for the staff on a regular basis. She recognizes the Moms on Mothers' Day, acknowledges the veterans on Veterans' Day and celebrates everybody's birthday with a small party in the office. She also brings in speakers in October for Breast Cancer Awareness and Domestic Violence month. She also develops programs for Black History Month, Women Month and other areas which may attract visitors and appeal to staff. She also gives her staff an opportunity to create a display in the museum to commemorate an event or holiday. The staff seem to enjoy each other, and they hardly have any issues. Gail encourages them to seek opportunities to improve themselves and she supports their every endeavor. She always says to her staff and to her family that, "Knowledge is Power, so Get You Some."

She is highly active in her sorority, Zeta Xi Zeta, holding several positions, including president throughout the years, and chairing several committees, including major fundraisers. She has been active with her sorority for over 20 years since she graduated from college. She often tells her friends and colleagues that the four years she spent in college was when she became the person she is today. She also says that being a member of a sorority was the icing on the cake. Not only was she able to join an organization that boasted high ideals in academic scholarship and endless efforts in community service, but she was able to meet sisters all over the country as she traveled to various meetings, events and conferences. Further, her membership continued after college, which many people thought sorority life was just a college thing. She believes in the mantra that membership has its privileges because she has benefitted from some of the most lasting and loving relationships she has ever made over the years.

In her neighborhood, she formed a Book Club called *The Paper Trailblazers*; they meet once a month at a different member's house. If it was at your house, you were responsible for lunch, libations and a closing thought-provoking game that dealt with the theme of the book. When the Book Club decided to get t-shirts, they changed their name to *Literal LOLers* of Dodge City; their subdivision was called Dodgewood Lakes, so they decided to continue the western theme by naming themselves after the popular city in the western television series, Gunsmoke. The LOL stands for Laugh Out Loud because they always end up in long laughing session after each meeting. One of the members designed the brown and yellow t-shirt which features a laughing emoji. The five ladies and three men would wear their t-shirts religiously whenever they went on cultural outings together. Another member would be sure to send a reminder via an online application that would pop up on their devices, especially in their texts, "Don't forget to wear your t-shirt next week." They especially loved attending the Zora Neale Hurston Festival every year in Eatonville, Florida in late January for a weekend of fun. They got to hear great lectures, listen to new music, eat good food and hang out with no worries for a few days. Although they officially met once a month, a few of them would get together when it was grocery store time or if someone wanted some company when running errands or making appointments.

Gail tries to workout at least two times a week before work at a gym near her job. A workout for her is 30 minutes on the elliptical, 30 minutes on the treadmill and 30 minutes to cool down. Because her hair is permed, she cannot do too much, because she does not want to look like a wet puppy when she goes to work. She thought about getting braids, but the last time she had her hair braided, the lady put clear polish at the end of each braid to keep it together and that just did not seem like a professional method. When she is having a bad hair day, her go-to styles are a ponytail, twists back to a ponytail or two braids. She is at an age, 42, where she is content. Lastly, she makes sure she has a "Date Night" every Thursday with Garrett, so they can concentrate on each other and catch up on family business without kid interruptions. They might go to the movies, or to a concert or to an event downtown, but mostly, they go out to dinner. This is where they can openly talk and listen to each other about work, family, dreams, and plans. Gail and Garrett choose on a rotating basis where they will go and what they will do each week. They agreed never to plan anything on Thursday nights because it is their time.

Gail was finally pulling up in the driveway. She had not been home in about three years; everything looked pretty much the same.

For the last three years everybody came to New Orleans for the holidays and they went on a cruise for their mother's last birthday. Just as she was about to get out of the car, her phone buzzed that she had a text message. It was her mother, "The key is in the mailbox, I'll be back in a few, got to check on a church member." Gail responded, "Ok, see you soon." She texted Adrianne, Angela, and Alex, "I am here at the house." Adrianne responded first, "Ok, I will see you in an hour or so." Angela texted, "I'll be by after work." Alex texted, "See you later alligator." Since it did not seem like anyone was coming any time soon, Gail headed towards the room where Adrianne said her items would be stored. She could not help but to visualize waking up in her twin bed, eating special dinners in the dining room, doing homework at the kitchen table, hanging laundry in the backyard, decorating for the holidays and playing games in the living room. Things were stacked up against the wall, boxes lined the hallway, clothes draped chairs, and everything seemed ready to move. At last, Gail spotted the cat collection in its display cases on the floor next to the china cabinet. She pulled out each one and examined it closely; they were in excellent condition. She put the cases on the couch near the front door. When she started to go back to the dining room, she saw a copy paper box marked in red, *Gail's Yearbooks and Tapes* near the entertainment center. Gail grabbed the box and sat it on the couch; there was her pink and blue cassette player on top. "I wonder if it still works," she said aloud. She grabbed the adapter, plugged it in the cassette player, found a nearby outlet, plugged it in and grabbed a cassette to pop in it. Each song would remind her of a significant event in her life.

Chapter 3

"Will it go round in circles? Will it fly high like a bird up in the sky..." Billy Preston

Brring...rring...Brring...rring. Gail! Get up Gail. It is time for school! Adrianne! Adrianne! Wake up Gail and get her ready for school. Adrianne was in the kitchen fixing breakfast. As she was stirring the grits, she said, "Okay Momma." She walked down the short-paneled hall to Gail and Alexandria's room. The paneled hall was lined with snapshots of Adrianne and Aldwin - professional pictures taken of them at the zoo, at school, etc. Her Mom said when the 3rd child came along, she could only afford to take the newborn and 1st year pictures. There were plenty of pictures of all the children, but Gail was the only one who noticed that there were more pictures of Adrianne and Aldwin than anyone else. She counted the pictures on that paneled wall.

There was one cute one of Gail when she got her new glasses, she was 10 years old and she was wearing a multi-print patchwork looking dress w/purple suede shoes. It was her absolute favorite outfit. It was on the wall, along with another with Angela in their Sunday yellow caped dresses. She liked that one too because they both looked like sweet little angels. There was a picture of her brother in a short white outfit that she also thought was really cute. Gail wondered what he was like as a little boy and often pretended that the boy in the picture was her *little* brother. She would talk to all the pictures on the wall and change her voice when answering as a different person. "Gail, you sure do look pretty in that yellow caped dress," she would say in a mature stern way like her Grandmother. "Well thank you Madear, it's my absolute favorite church dress," she would respond in the sweetest way. "Butter would not melt in this child's mouth; she was so sweet." Her Grandmother would add, "You look like a little angel." This would go on for minutes as one of Gail's favorite pastimes while waiting on someone to come out of the bathroom or for someone to notice her. If anyone was ever looking for Gail, she would mostly likely be in the hallway.

"Gail, get up!" Adrianne bellowed. "Everybody else is up and getting ready to go. Get up." Adrianne pulled the baby blue floral-patterned bedspread off Gail. Gail's orange scarf was slightly off her head, but her hairstyle was still intact and would need only a little brushing. Gail had sandy brown hair and it always looked like it was dirty, but that was just its color. She was a small frame child with bony legs. She pulled the cover over her head and yelled, "Ma!" "Gail, just get up," her Mom piped in to divert a confrontation. Gail slowly got up and her Cinderella pajamas were hanging off her like a pole holding up a tent with one stake missing. Her pajamas were hand-me-downs from Angela. Most of her wardrobe was hand-me-downs, because her Mom made sure they took care of their clothes. Everyday after school, they would have to take off their school clothes and put on their play clothes before going outside. Gail would have the most extensive wardrobe because she had new outfits, plus whatever her sisters passed down to her.

She was the youngest of five children and she hated it because everybody told her what to do. She hated being called the *baby* and corrected people to say she was the youngest. She also reminded people to call her Gail and not her formal sounding name, April. The older guys called her, dirty red, because her hair always looked dirty, when she walked to the store or to the mailbox. She was all legs, flat-chested and very thin. All the children were born at John Gaston Hospital in Memphis; this is also the hospital where their mother ended up working. They moved onto North Dunbar Street in the Summer of 1977 on July 4th. Her oldest brother, Aldwin had just graduated from high school in May. Her sisters, Adrianne, Alexandria, and Angela were all two years apart and they all looked alike. Their mother put Adrianne and Angela in a room and Alexandria and Gail in a room. She put an older girl with a younger girl so they could have some guidance. Adrianne combed Gail's and Angela's hair and picked their clothes for school when their Mom was working or just too tired. She cooked just like their mother and everybody respected her and did what she said without question. Alexandria was the *troublesome* one. She was only interested in boys and the boys wanted her too. She was the 1st girl to need a bra, because as *Madear* said she was "top heavy." Angela was a petite little girl with a mean streak about her. She would often beat up kids who messed with Gail. She was very protective of her baby sister.

Everybody loved the house and the neighborhood. Since Gail's parents were divorced when she was so young, she was never sad or jealous when her friends talked about their fathers. In fact, many of her friends had fathers, but it did not bother her at all. She was always quick to say, "You cannot miss what you never had." The girls liked when their mother worked the 7 a.m. to 3 p.m. shift best of all, because she would get home about the same time as they did from school and they would all have dinner together and share their days like the families they watched on television. Most times Adrianne would cook, but when their mother felt like cooking, she would also make a special dessert like banana pudding or caramel cake. Each girl had a job to do at dinner time: someone would set the table, someone would make the beverage, someone would put ice in glasses, and someone would make the plates. It was quite a production that ended with mother saying grace. Once everybody finished eating, cleared the table and washed the dishes, they would usually play a game. They would play a board game like Monopoly or a home-made game. Most preferred the home-made game because it often had monetary prizes. Sometimes you could win a chore-free week; that was a good prize, too. If they did not play a game, Gail would grab the Sears catalog and circle everything she wanted for school with a red pen. She would also write each catalog order number on a pad in case they had a cash windfall and all she would have to do is pick up the phone and place the order to The Sears Catalog Center. She would also ask her sisters what they wanted, and she would jot down those catalog numbers, too. Then Gail would say, "Momma, what do you want?"

Gail slowly crept down the hall to the bathroom. "Hurry up Gail," her mother called out from the bedroom. "You're not going to have time to eat, if you keep moving so slow." Her mother knew her child's every motion without leaving her bedroom. Gail perked up and moved in and out of the bathroom quickly. She darted down the hall to the kitchen and plopped in a red chair at the round red table.

The modest kitchen was small but quaint. Their mother had painstakingly saved *Quality Stamps* to buy the red, blue & yellow striped *Priscilla* curtains with matching dish towels, throw rug and cloth place mats. The red strawberries in the pattern made the table and chairs look very elegant. The top kitchen drawer was full of *Quality Stamp* books; her mother would check it ever so often to see what she could buy. She was immensely proud of the curtain set and was often fussing over it like someone's new dress. She would brush off dust and gently slide them over on the rod when she wanted to open the window. "My grits are cold and there are just crumbs of bacon left," Gail whined to the air. Everybody was getting their books together and doing last minute checks and touches on their hair and clothes. This was their 1st day at a new school, and they wanted to look good. "Too bad, so sad," Adrianne yelled out from the living room. Angela added, "Too bad, so sad," and Alexandria said, "Hurry up." "Momma, tell Gail to hurry up." Gail ran down the hall to the living room before her mother got up. She could hear the mattress springs creaking. "Okay, okay," Gail said as she pulled the scarf off her head. She ate a few spoonsful of grits and grabbed the pieces of bacon left, eating it all very quickly. "I'm coming,"

Gail said. She gulped down the small glass of orange juice and ran down the hall.

Adrianne had combed her hair last night and all she had to do was put barrettes at the end of each braided ponytail. Gail started to run to the bedroom to get the barrettes, but Adrianne was holding them out in her hand. "Are you looking for these?" "Thanks, big Sis – You take such good care of your little sister, don't you." Adrianne pulled Gail's head towards her and started putting the barrettes on her ponytails. She smiled because she loved getting the praise for this thankless job. "I've got the nicest big sister," Gail pined, "I've got the prettiest big sister…" "Okay, okay, *Rhoda*, do not do the *Bad Seed* script please, Adrianne said. *The Bad Seed* is a 1956 movie starring a mischievous blonde pig-tailed donning little girl named Rhoda. She kills her classmate, Claude over a penmanship medal that she felt she should have won. Whenever it seemed as though her Mom was getting closer to the truth, she would turn on the charm. "I've got the nicest mother. I've got the prettiest mother." It is a thriller because Rhoda is so good, and you just cannot imagine that she is so bad. Adrianne added, "I hope you will not imitate everything Rhoda did in the movie. We all know what happened to her." Adrianne brushed Gail's hair in spots where it was coming loose and then patted her on her back so she could go and get her things together. "Hurry up," everybody said in unison.

They were finally ready to go. Adrianne and Alexandria were going to walk Gail and Angela to Middle School. The high school was right next door. Gail was in the 6th grade and she could hardly wait until she could meet her teachers, see her classmates, join clubs, and eat lunch in the new cafeteria. The cafeteria was renovated in the summer because they found mold in the wall behind the sitting area. A student was pushing tables together and accidentally knocked a hole in the wall. When the maintenance crew went to patch it up, they discovered the mold. Angela was in the 8th grade and she was a cheerleader. She always had a lot of friends with her walking home. They were mostly cheerleaders and athletes, but they all seemed to be a close-knit bunch. She was immensely popular, and Gail wanted that same notoriety. Angela loved cheering during basketball season; she did not care to be outside in the cold or rain during football season. Her mother told her it was her job to cheer the team to victory, so the weather should not keep her from having school spirit. Angela did not pursue cheerleading in high school. Gail decided she would try out for cheerleader in high school.

Chapter 4

Gail's 6th grade teacher, Mrs. T. S. Dotson was a petite lady in her late 30s. She seemed nice until she started to talk about everything they were going to do that school year – essays, language projects, speeches, dioramas, plays and more. There were 24 kids in the class, 15 girls and 9 boys. Gail sat next to a girl who introduced herself as Vida. Vida was a skinny girl with orange-red thick hair pulled back into a bun. She wore a green overall dress with a paisley short-sleeve shirt and some tan oxfords with knee socks. She looked like a black Swiss Miss; she was from Alaska. They found out that they lived in the same neighborhood, so they agreed to meet after school and walk home together. Mrs. Dotson asked if anyone had a ruler in their school supply bags and Gail was quick to say, "Yes, at home." It was clear that Mrs. Dotson was perturbed from this outburst. She asked, "Who said that?" Gail quickly raised her hand. Mrs. Dotson asked her to stand; she then asked Gail why she would volunteer an item that is not available at this moment. "Do you understand the question," Mrs. Dotson asked. "Uh-huh, yea - sorry," Gail answered. Mrs. Dotson walked up to Gail and said, "Young lady, when you respond to me, it will be Yes Ms. Dotson or No Mrs. Dotson, Do you understand?" Gail repeated, "Yes, Mrs. Dotson.

Gail sat quietly and wondered, "who was this lady, Mrs. T. S. Dotson?" She put Gail in her place, and she did not like it, but she was intrigued by her tenacity. Gail looked at Mrs. Dotson's desk. It was organized with file folders, books, worksheets, pens, and paper.

There was not a pen out of place; everything was in its proper place. As Gail looked around the classroom, she noticed everything was neat, colorful, and appealing. Mrs. Dotson had been teaching at the middle school for ten years and she had a reputation of being firm, but fair. Gail also noticed Mrs. Dotson's briefcase, portfolio, and lunch bag – they all had some strange letters on them that started with a Z and ended with a Z. As she looked closer, she could see that her portfolio had the words Zeta Xi Zeta Sorority on it; she did not know what it meant, but she liked the orange and blue colors. Then she realized the classroom had orange and blue accents probably because of this Zeta Xi Zeta club. Gail began to watch Mrs. Dotson very closely and soon she began to admire her for her knowledge and ability. Gail began to look at Mrs. Dotson differently; she was a good looking lady with a small frame and an eye for smart fashion. Her black hair was short and cropped to accentuate her face and she wore dark framed glasses. She looked like the perfect teacher and Gail could easily claim Mrs. Dotson as her favorite teacher. Gail thought, "this lady deserved my respect and I'm going to give it to her."

"Class, listen up," Mrs. Dotson said as she walked up and down the aisles. As she walked, she motioned for students to sit up. She said, "sit up, feet flat, chest out, and in the center." She told the class they would be seated according to their grades; the 1st seat will be for the person with the highest average and so on. She proceeded to pass out a work sheet face down. "Do not turn this paper over until I say so. "This will determine the seating for the next two weeks until you start earning grades." Mrs. Dotson said, "You may begin – you have 20 minutes." There were 10 math problems at the top and 10 fill-in-the-blank sentences at the bottom. Gail did not think it was too difficult; she ended up sitting in chair five and her friend, Vida was right behind her in chair six - that suited her simply fine. They felt rather good to be in the top ten. The top four seats went to Sherry Dreiser, Keith Eastland, Lisa Landers, and Gwendolyn Worth. They did not miss any questions, so Ms. Dotson put them in alphabetical order. Gail felt bad for the boy who was in the last seat. His name was Travis Smallwood, but everybody called him Soul Train. She waved at him from seat 5 just to be funny. He did not wave back to her and he did not think she was funny.

Shirley Dreiser was a cross between Dolly Parton and Loretta Lynn – she was tall, thin and she had wild bushy blondish-brown hair. She loved Elvis and she proudly proclaimed that she was his #1 fan. She had the loudest snorting laugh; when you made her laugh, you had better be prepared to laugh with her. She was very emotional; she was either incredibly happy or incredibly sad. She confided in us that it was just her and her Mom at home. She said being an only child was very lonely. Shirley's mother, Helen, was a factory worker and she loved working in her yard. She would always send Mrs. Dotson flowers from her garden. You could tell Shirley was embarrassed by her Mom when she came to visit or attend programs. She would slink down in her chair or her posture would noticeably change. Her Mom did not dress the best, and her hair and clothes always seemed as though she had just come through a windstorm. Mrs. Dotson always tried to make Shirley's Mom feel welcome and comfortable by giving her extra attention prior to the program. She would ask her about gardening. "Ms. Helen, I can't seem to grow anything right now," Mrs. Dotson would say. "What do you recommend for this season?" Helen's face would light up with excitement to talk about something she knew about passionately. "Mrs. Dotson, I'll tell you what would bloom pretty good with little work," she would say with a smile.

Keith Eastland was a large boy with freckles and thick super straight hair. Gail thought she noticed a slight mustache when she passed him to get to seat five. She could not tell if he was Native American, Lebanese or Latina – nobody asked, either. He was not very talkative, but as the year went by, they became fast friends. He was the boy Mrs. Dotson would always ask to assist with moving chairs or tables if they were having a program, a class party or if she was decorating the classroom. He was extremely helpful and did not mind helping in other classrooms, as well. Teachers would pop in and ask Mrs. Dotson, "May we borrow Keith for a few minutes?" Mrs. Dotson would gladly oblige. Keith rode the bus so he always left 15 minutes before school was out, "Those students riding the bus, please head to the hallway," the Principal would make this announcement every day on the intercom.

Lisa Landers acted like a little mouse; she did not want you to see her. She was a skinny girl with straightened brown hair that was parted and stretched into two ponytails. She had pink yarn on each ponytail tied into a nice bow. It matched her pink sweater perfectly and Gail wondered if someone made it for her. She had on a brown top and a brown skirt that seemed too big. Gail thought she probably had big sisters like her and was wearing hand-me-downs. Lisa was quiet, she did not talk directly to you, and did look directly at you. She talked like she was telling you a secret. She covered her mouth when she talked or laughed like she had bad breath or bad teeth. She did not have either of these issues; she was a shy girl who lacked noticeable confidence. She was a genius in math. When Lisa walked, it was if she did not want to go because her gait was at a hesitating pace. Mrs. Dotson sent the top three students to the board to do some math problems and she whizzed through those problems with little difficulty. Everybody clapped each time she finished before everybody else. It was like a math contest and Lisa was the winner! Mrs. Dotson said Lisa had a natural gift for seeing the numbers, seeing the problems, and finding the solution. Gail knew she wanted to be Lisa's friend because she seemed sweet and because she was not good in math.

Gwendolyn Worth was a regal looking little girl. She stood tall and carried herself in a manner that lead you to believe that she came from a well-bred family. She wore her hair down with a yellow ribbon for headband; it had a familiar smell – sulfur. Gail recognized that smell from her neighbors across the street. It is supposed to make your hair grow, so she did not shun Gwen because of her hair smell. She had a wider girth than the other girls, but she was neat in her appearance. She had on the cutest sunflower adorned dress with white sandals. It turns out she was the only girl in the class that wore a bra, so she was standing tall because she was adapting to wearing it; it was hurting her shoulders and back. When she was at the board doing math problems, she told everybody her favorite subject was science. Mrs. Dotson said she would be sure to let Gwen take the lead when science project time came around in the spring.

Finally, the first day of school was over at 3:00 p.m. It was a good day and Gail thought she would make some lifelong friends. Gail and Vida talked outside of school for a few minutes to get an idea of which route to take to get home. Vida's house was closest, so they decided to walk down the street that would connect to her street first. Suddenly, the boy named *Soul Train* came up to them and interrupted their conversation. "five and six, y'all think you're smart, huh?" The girls ignored him and turned their backs. Soul Train hollered to his buddies, "Let's get them!" Gail and Vida started to run. When Vida saw her street, she waved and kept running towards her house. Gail continued to run with the boys close behind. Gail came running down her street and the boys soon disappeared. She could not believe that the boys led by *Soul Train*, chased Vida and her over a seating joke. With a name like Soul Train, you would think he would be a fun person who likes to dance.

Gail's mother was on the porch shelling purple hull peas. "Slow down, how was school?" Her mother asked again, "How was school?" Gail was out of breath, but she managed to say in between panting, "these boys were chasing us." Her mother sat up, "What –what boys?" "Why were they chasing you?" Her mother listened intently as Gail recalled her day at school. Gail's mother moved the beans from her lap and stood up looking up and down the street. "They're gone now," Gail said. "When we got to our street, they disappeared down an alley – Vida, that's the girl I met in my class; she ran one way and I ran the other." Angela was coming out the door with a glass of lemonade and some graham crackers. "What happened," she asked anxiously. Gail told her some boys from her class chased her and a friend home from school. Angela did not want anybody messing with her little sister, so she was gearing up to go and beat them up. You could see her engine revving up as she asked Gail to point them out tomorrow. "For real, I want you to point them out, okay," Angela said. Gail hesitantly said, "Okay." Mother said, "Don't you go and try and pick a fight with those little boys…Do you hear me?" "Yes ma'am," replied Angela. "Where's Adrianne?" their mother asked. "She needs to help me finish dinner; my head is starting to hurt from all this drama. They watched their mother walk down the driveway, out of earshot for a minute, looking for Adrianne. "Momma's head is always hurting," said Gail. "Do you think she has a brain tumor?" she asked Angela. "No, she does not have a tumor; you watch too much television. She just works too hard at work and needs to rest more," Angela said.

"Adrianne," Their mother shouted while walking back up the driveway to the porch. She picked up the bowl of peas and headed inside the house. "Y'all pick up this paper and put it in the trash can," their mother insisted. "Yes ma'am," they said in unison. Nobody liked purple hull peas, except their mother, so why she took all the time to shell them, nobody knew exactly. Later we found out it was very therapeutic and relaxing for her. While shelling peas, their mother would sit on the porch and watch the happenings on Dunbar Street. It was a good diversion from thinking about doctors, nurses, patients, medicine, and work. She especially liked listening to the sister and brother that lived directly across the street. They were the last white folks on the block; they had been there for 25 years. They sat on their porch most evenings after dinner.

Chapter 5

Well I don't know why I came here tonight; I got the feeling that something ain't right..." Stealers Wheel

Glenn and Margie Conway were the neighbors across the street. The sister, who was in her mid 60's moved in with the brother who was in his early 70's to help take care of him. Gail's mother called it "white flight" because when we started moving in, white folks started moving out. Gail's mother said it was their loss that they did not give us a chance to get to know them. "If they do not want to take the time to get to know me as a neighbor, then it is too bad for them," she said. Glenn and Margie wore hearing aids, so they talked very loudly to each other. When they sat on the porch, the whole street could hear their conversation. Gail's mother especially enjoyed listening to their bickering, chatting and diatribes. She said it was like watching a soap opera. There was drama because the kids never came to visit, and they talked about that a lot. There was suspense because you never knew what they were going to fuss about for the day. During the holidays, they would always make the children of the neighborhood goody bags filled with special treats. There were about 20 kids on the street ranging from ages from 4 to 17, so they enjoyed handing out treats. Margie loved to bake, and Glenn loved to do woodwork. One year for Easter, Glenn made little wooden baskets and Margie put 3 egg-shaped cookies wrapped in yellow and pink tissue inside the basket. The kids spoke to the Conway's from afar, rode their bikes quickly by the house, went up to their porch to get their treats and hurried off with a thank you in transit. Margie Conway would often go to the bottom of her step and hold out a tray and the kids would rush over like bees to honey. One day it might be popcorn balls, another day it would be butter cookies and sometimes the tray would be loaded with candy: *Butterfingers, 3 Musketeers, Paydays, Chico-sticks,* and *Stage-planks.* Margie Conway would say, "Brother and I can't have any sweets, so take 'em all." You did not have to tell them twice; the tray was empty within minutes once the word spread. "Mrs. Margie got candy," they would shout. Nobody really liked or disliked them; they were just this odd couple on the street who did nice things for the children. They were basically harmless and weird at the same time. Adrianne worked at the corner store 3 days a week, so Mrs. Margie would bring over a few treats just for her. If she did not see everybody, she would always put a few treats aside. "I'll save these last ones for later, tell your brothers and sisters to come and get a treat," she would insist.

All the Conway family members appeared to be out of town; they seldom had visitors. All they had was each other; they tolerated each other. They raked leaves together and helped keep up the yard together. They even walked to the mailbox and corner store together. When they finally settled down, with a tray of apple cider, cheddar cheese and vanilla wafers, you could hear their whole conversation – they affectionately called each other brother and sister.

"Brother, do you think it was right for that salesperson at *The Treasury* to brush me off so quickly?" "Sister, we had been in there for over an hour and you couldn't make up your mind on what you wanted," he said annoyingly. "Well, isn't that her job?" Mrs. Conway balked in rudely. "She's supposed to help me." "Sister, she had other people to help, not just you." "Well, brother, you know that's why I didn't buy anything," she growled. "You specifically said you wanted to buy a jewelry box for one of the kids as a graduation present." Mrs. Conway loudly added, "Well, I will not get it from there with the bad service." "Okay, okay," Mr. Conway said as he got up from the swing. It seemed like they were always arguing or disagreeing about something.

On Valentine's Day, Mrs. Conway would make cookies with red and pink frosting; everyone thought they were better than any store-bought cookie. At Halloween, they would pass out popcorn balls and fill goody bags with the best candy. They would include those peanut butter taffy-like chews, Mary Janes. People would buy that orange and black candy thinking the kids liked it and the kids would just throw them away. Who likes that candy? At Christmas time, Mr. Conway would make some type of wooden ornament in shapes like trees, doves, bells, stars, etc. Everybody on Dunbar street had something from the Conways in their house.

Chapter 6

Oh yes I am wise but it's wisdom born of pain. Yes,
I've paid the price, but look how much I gained..."
Helen Reddy

"Where is Adrianne," Their mother shouted from the front door. The girls ran into the living room where their mother was sitting on the couch. "Mr. Cathy called and asked if she could work today and she ran down there," Gail said. "She didn't ask me," mother said. Angela said, "You were in the backyard hanging out some clothes when he called Momma." "Angela, bring me his phone number off the refrigerator and then bring me the phone," Momma said as she folded her arms across her chest. "Yes ma'am," Angela said as she hurried off to find the number. "Folks get a job and then they're grown," she said under her breath. "She's not too old for me to whip..." "Here's the number, Momma," Angela said. "Thank you, baby. Let's see, Wallace Cathy's Corner Store, 525-9911." She dialed the number. The girls watched and listened patiently as they approached the couch to sit near their mother. While she was dialing the number, Gail noticed that her mother had a streak of gray hair on the top of her head. She had never noticed it before. Her mother had a beautiful smooth caramel face with a few small moles on it; they looked like freckles. She was a 36-year-old woman with a nice shape for a woman with 5 children. She was probably a size 16, but she was proportioned well, not flabby at all. She was always wearing

28

some type of house dress because she wanted to be comfortable when she came home from the hospital. She would take off her nurse's uniform, take a bath and put on a crispy clean house dress; she had about 6 of them. On her birthday, somebody would always get her one and it would be purple or a shade of purple, her favorite color. The one she was wearing today had tangerines, oranges, grapes, apples, and oranges on a pastel purple background. Gail called it Momma's "fruity" dress. Her hair was short and curly; it was always pressed and curled.

She married too early to the wrong man and she knew it, but it was the only way out of the house back in the day. Her children were the best thing she got out of the divorce. She loved being with her children and she showered them with attention and affection. She took an interest in everything they did, whether it was in the neighborhood or in school. If they were reading a book for school, she would read it too. They would have discussions about the book – she especially liked Toni Morrison's <u>The Bluest Eye</u> and Harper Lee's <u>To Kill a Mockingbird</u>. She also loved playing board games like Monopoly, Scrabble, Concentration and Pay Day. The game the kids liked most of all would be the games she made up. There was one where she would cut up colored squares of paper, write different chores or tasks on them and place them in a jar or basket - like: *sweep the kitchen floor* or *give your sister a hug*. Sometimes you would get lucky and pick a square that said, you just earned $1 for being special. The game would go on until all the squares were gone from the jar. The house would be clean, and we would be happy with our rewards of hugs, bubblegum, kisses, quarters, or candy.

"Hello, is this Mr. Cathy? Yes, but next time, please check with me to see if it's okay for Adrianne to work. She is a child and can not make those decisions about working. Thank you, but if she has homework, she'll have to get off at 8:00 p.m." Her mother held the phone back and waited as she heard him asking Adrianne if she had homework. "Ms. Quincy, she said she does not have any homework," Mr. Cathy said. "Please put my child on the phone Mr. Cathy," she insisted. "Hello Momma," said Adrianne. "Adrianne, I'll talk to you when you get home at 8:05 – love you. She hung up the phone when she heard Adrianne say, "yes ma'am." "I guess that means Adrianne's not helping with dinner," Angela whispered to Gail. "I'll help with dinner," Gail enthusiastically said. "Me too Momma," Angela added. "Okay girls, let's get dinner started." "Where's Alex," their mother looked at them puzzlingly. They said in unison, "I don't know." Both knew that while their mother was taking the peas into the house, they saw Alex flirting with Terrence, Bertha's cousin. Bertha was Alex's best friend and it seems she had hundreds of cousins always coming to visit. "Come on let's get cooking – these peas will have to cook a couple of hours. We can play a game while they are cooking. Maybe Adrianne will get home just in time for dinner and she can make a dessert; that girl loves to cook sweets. I thought I loved cooking sweets, but she has me beat." They headed towards the living room. "What game do you want to play Momma," Gail asked. "Let's play Scrabble!"

Chapter 7

No one else can make me feel the colors that you bring. Stay with me while we grow old and we will live each day in springtime..."Minnie Ripperton

"Come on Alexandria, it won't take long. Just ride with me downtown." Alex looked sheepishly at Terrence and said, "Why so formal, call me Alex - Will I be back by dinner time at 7?" "Of course, you will, it's just 6 o'clock, now," Terrence responded. Terrence was so happy to be driving his Mom's 1975 Monte Carlo; it was burgundy inside and out. The darkness of the car and its interior excited them both. Alex thought Terrence was very cool because he was driving, and he was from East Memphis. He looked like he was 25, but he was only 17. He was a tall, dark, thin guy with a short haircut. His ears were the first things Alex noticed when she first met him; he looked like he could fly away with those Dumbo-ears, she told Bertha. He also had the cutest dimples; they were so deep and inviting, you could get lost in them for days. Alex loved when Terrence came to Bertha's house to hang out with her brother Bailey. Sometimes Terrence's Mom would let him have the car for the entire weekend and he would pick up all his "fellas" to joyride. Terrence lived in East Memphis with his Mom, Dad and 2 sisters. Before he could drive, his Mom would drop him off at Bertha's on her way to work. She worked 3:00 – 11:00 shifts at the nearby hospital as a ward clerk. Her girls were independent at 14 years old and 12 years old, so they could stay home by themselves without getting into any trouble. Terrence, on the other hand, needed to be monitored more closely. When he stayed home with his sisters, he would aggravate them to tears or fighting. He would constantly nag at them saying they were boring, and he would try to convince them to go places. Their mother told them not to leave the house, so they were not going anywhere. He fought with Tasha, his 14-year-old sister most of all. His mother got tired of Zhariah, the 12-year-old, calling her at the hospital; she would have to leave work to go and break up the fight. Terrence would also have all his friends over, eating up all the food, *sucking up all the air* and *bogarding* the television. Zhariah would call and tell that too. So, his Mom, Ms. Jewel decided to bring Terrence to his Aunt's house for safekeeping on her way to work. Terrence's Dad, Ernest, was a landscaper who worked all hours of the day and was in and out infrequently. His Dad suggested Terrence go to his sister, Betty's house in South Memphis. There boys were the same age and they genuinely liked each other.

"*Ooh, baby, I think I love you from head to toe...*" Lisa Lisa & Cult Jam

"That's not the way home," Alex noticed. "Let's just go to the park for a few minutes," Terrence pleaded. "I promise I'll have you home by 7 pm! Terrence clasped both his hands together in a praying position and gave her a silly smile. "Okay, okay, put your hands back on the wheel and wipe that puppy dog grin off your face," Alex ordered. Terrence was a good driver and Alex liked watching him drive and maneuver the car. The Monte Carlo was a stick shift and it was something about watching him change gears that was very intriguing and sexy. She could ride with him for hours. Terrence parked the car near the merry-go-round and asked Alex if she wanted to take a ride. Alex jumped out of the car, ran towards the merry-go-round and Terrence ran after her. Alex got to the merry-go-round first and sat on the edge letting her feet propel her around. When Terrence arrived, he began to push her faster and faster until she was but a whirl in motion. He jumped on as the merry-go –round lost momentum; when it stopped, they dizzily bumped into each other and fell. It appeared to be an accident, but a touching moment, none the less. "Did you just fall for me?" Terrence looked at Alex as she lay flat on the merry-go-round with her legs flailing over the edge. "Hey girl, I asked you a question – did you just fall for me?" Alex sat up slowly with stars in her eyes and said, "I guess so." Terrence jumped off the merry-go-round, bent down to where Alex was and lifted her up in his arms; he gave her a simple peck on the lips. They looked at each other intensely as though this were their last chance for a moment like this and began to kiss more passionately. They kissed like they were shooting a scene from the soap opera, of *All My Children*; he was bad boy, *Jesse* and she was good girl, *Angie*. Neither admitted that this was their first kiss, but they just pretended that the other person knew what they were doing. Alex thought, "it felt good, so it must be right." Terrence thought to himself, "I cannot believe I'm kissing her." Still kissing, Alex felt her leg dragging with the merry-go-round – Terrence noticed and pulled her closer to him. They stood there, close – nose to nose, dusty from the merry-go-round dirt in the dark. Then they felt the merry-go-round moving around. They looked around to see how it started and they saw Alex's brother, Aldwin. "Does Momma know you're here," he bellowed. Alex yelled back, "Does Momma know you're here? Aldwin was there with his friend, Arthur. The two of them had been friends since they were in kindergarten and even before that – they did everything together. Many people thought they were brothers because they looked so much alike. Since Aldwin did not have any brothers, Arthur was the next best thing to having a brother.

The brother and sister looked at each other and gave a quick smirk. Arthur jumped in, "Man, both of y'all need to get home before it gets too late." Terrence looked at Arthur like he was etching *Stay out of my business* on his forehead. Arthur looked back at Terrence in a *I don't know what you're looking at me for* look.

Arthur always had a crush on Alex, but she never gave him a second look. To her, he was like a brother. Once, while they were playing in the backyard, they got close to a kiss. Alex was 10 and Arthur was 14. Alex was trying to show Gail, who was 7 at the time, how to make the perfect mud pie. Alex decided to hold a cooking class and made Gail and Angela sit on the ground at attention. The girls had their piles of mud on a wooden board. They also had grass, rocks, and sticks for garnishments. Arthur and Aldwin were tossing a football nearby. Alex began to teach her class. Take a handful of mud and toss it back and forth until it is no longer watery. Take a smidgen of grass and mix it with the mud. Start tossing it again and pat it into a nice round circle. The girls were covered in the splattered mud mixture, but they enjoyed the attention from their big sister. While their mud-grass concoction was drying in the sun, they decided to play house. Of course, Alex was the Mom and Angela and Gail were her daughters. Alex pretended to have them picking cotton in the field while she sat on the porch shelling peas. Suddenly, the football landed right near her foot. Alex took that as a cue – "My goodness Arthur Honey, watch it with that football." She continued in the role while Arthur inhaled the moment, she called him *Honey.* "Your girls are out in the fields picking cotton. I am going to knit you a nice fluffy pillow with that yellow and orange yarn when I finish shelling these peas. Would you like that?" Arthur beamed. "Arthur are you going to throw the ball some time today," Aldwin shouted. "Honey, you go on back and play football with your friend. We really need to find him a wife, don't we?" Alex and Arthur smiled at each other. Arthur thought he would take advantage of the moment. "How about a kiss goodbye, Dear?" Alex leaned over to give him peck when her mother yelled, "What are y'all doing looking like little dirt rags out there?" She walked towards the girls first while Arthur backed away. He gripped the football, peeved about the interruption, tossed it to Aldwin. Aldwin sent it back long and hard. He shouted, "Throw it like Larry Csonka, not like Leslie Csonka. Arthur snapped out of his love-struck stupor and began throwing the ball correctly.

Gail and Angela were being stripped as they walked towards the house. "How in the world could you have gotten so muddy and dirty in such a short time? I will put you both in the tub. I'll even put some of my bath cubes in the water." The girls smiled because they loved the way their mother smelled when she had a nice long bath using those bath cubes – they loved anything off their mother's dresser. She had a huge mirror sitting on her dresser and she had all types of lipsticks, lotions, nail polish and perfumes; they were arranged so elegantly on a silver tray.

"Alex, come in the house and find your sisters some clean underwear and clothes," her mother shouted. Alex hurried towards the house following her mother's voice. "You might as well get their PJs since it's so close to bedtime." Alex sneaked a peak back at Arthur and smiled briefly. She huffed and puffed all the way to the house. Arthur had been in love with Alex ever since that day. He was very protective of her and would not let anybody talk about her. Whenever he came to the house to see Aldwin, he would always ask, where are the girls? Aldwin would rattle off who was where, but Arthur was only listening for Alex's whereabouts.

"Arthur! Arthur!" Aldwin shouted, where is your mind? "Aw man, I was just thinking of this cutie-pie I met a while back." "Hey, let's ask Terrence if we can get a ride," said Aldwin. "Can we catch a ride home with you?" said Arthur and Aldwin. "Where is your car," Terrence asked? "It is still in Arthur's garage suffering from need-repair-itis. Can we catch a ride with you or not, man?" insisted Aldwin. Alex sat in front with Terrence while the boys sat in the back checking the dashboard from afar. Arthur screamed above the scratchy radio, "Man, tell your Momma to put some serious speakers in this car." Arthur held up a crocheted pillow – "what is this?" Terrence bellowed, "My sister Daphne made that for my Momma. Sometimes she needs a pillow for her back while she's driving." "Maybe you should not step on so many cracks, Arthur chuckled. Aldwin added, "Step on a crack, break your Momma's back." Terrence winced, "that's not even funny."

Chapter 8

"...You will find peace of mind if you look way down in your heart and soul. Don't hesitate 'cause the world seems cold ..."Earth, Wind & Fire

Aldwin was all packed for Marine boot camp in Paris Island, SC. He sat in his room having flash backs of everything and everybody. When he graduated last year, he worked odd jobs here and there, but that just did not cut it. He wanted more; he studied all the preparation guides for the ASVAB (Armed Services Vocational Aptitude Battery) and made top scores to enter the Marines. Even though the threat of going to war in Vietnam was a possibility, he did not feel afraid. He was anxious for the adventure the Marines offered, especially since his grades were not good enough to get a college scholarship. He wanted to make his mother proud by making something of himself. He wanted to be proud of himself. Everybody was rushing around the house busy with activity. Mother was just finishing icing a coffee cake and Adrianne was peeling potatoes nearby. Alexandria was in the backroom talking to Arthur. She and Arthur were very much in love, but her Mom wanted her to finish high school. They made plans to marry after high school, the Summer after graduation. It was May 3rd and they only had a few weeks to wait until graduation, May 24th. Alex was visibly pregnant, and their baby was due in August. Her Mom had promised to keep her 11a to 7p shift so Alex could go to college and she would watch the baby. Arthur went with Alex to all her prenatal doctor's appointments. He was very attentive to her needs and doted on her continuously. "So where are we going to live," Alex asked. Arthur stood up, as if to give a speech of something. "'We are going to live in The Westbury Apartments on North Parkway. We can go look at them tomorrow; I am just waiting on your final approval. They are nice, and the area is quiet. It will be close to my job at the Board of Education and I can come home for lunch sometimes. "You have all things thought out," Alex pined in. "I love a man who takes charge – what else baby?" Arthur made good money as a truck driver taking supplies and equipment to the city schools. He was also going to a technical school to learn a trade - plumbing. "Well, we have our choice of an upstairs apartment or a downstairs apartment – with a balcony or without. I wouldn't want you to get tired going up and down stairs, but I want you to feel safe while I'm away." "We will make all of those decisions tomorrow, today is Aldwin's day – it's all about him," Alex said.

"Alex!" mother shouted. Her mother headed to the backroom. She was wearing a multi-print housedress that seemed much too big. She was wearing perspiration like someone had sprayed her with a water bottle. Her hair was pulled back and pinned up with bobby pins. Alex and Arthur were sitting closely on the couch smooching. "Isn't this how you got this way, pointing at Alex's stomach, in the first place, hanging out back here?" Alex and Arthur looked at each other and smiled; they were embarrassed, but happy. "Well, it's done now, I need some help." Arthur jumped up, "But Momma Quincy, she's so far long, shouldn't she be still?" "Arthur, she's pregnant, not dying." Mother said pregnant like the word could not completely come out the right way – she could not say menstruation or penis without an awkward disposition either. Pregnant was a word that she felt was not to be said out loud and certainly not with mixed company; it was obvious she was uncomfortable every time she said it. Alex slowly rose with some help from Arthur. She gave out a big moan like a hippo stretching after wallowing in a slushy mire.

She was always overly dramatic with everything; this was not any different. "Come on girl, I need you to get the living room cleaned up." Mother walked away and then slowly looked back. "Arthur, why don't you go and see Aldwin." "Yes ma'am," Arthur said. "I'm going to miss my play brother, heck he has been like a real brother to me. I know the Marines will take good care of him."

Chapter 9

"Just Stop 'cause I really love you, Stop, I'll be thinking of you. Look in my heart and let love keep us together, what ever...." The Captain and Tennille

Gail sat on the porch out of the way of all the commotion. She looked up and down Dunbar Street and wondered if any other house had such excitement as hers. She would miss her brother; he was annoying at times, but he would always take up for her when others would mess with her. He would sometimes affectionately call her, *baby sister* when he needed her to fold his clothes or bring him a cool drink. She thought about the good times she had with her brother. Maybe he would send her postcards from all his travels or even some souvenirs. Gail thought it was fantastic that Aldwin got to go on this military adventure, not realizing the danger of it all.

Directly across the street was Ms. Joanie's house. She had 4 daughters and twin sons. Her house was not as big, but it looked like a home – lived in and worn. All her grass was now dirt from her children going back and forth with bikes, skates, etc. Gail's mother would not let them play with the children much because she said they always used bad English and foul language. The girls, ages 12, 10, 7 and 6 were tomboys; they never jumped rope, played jacks, or played with dolls. They were always racing down the street, wrestling in the yard or talking loudly about other people. The twins, Eric and Derek were only 4 years old, but they had a vast vocabulary.

One day Eric told Derek that he was "absolutely sure I can kick your butt without blinking." Their mother was a major *One Life to Live* fan, which was her favorite soap opera. Everybody on the street knew where she was during that hour and if you were walking by the house, you could hear the television volume turned up extremely high. Sometimes you could hear Ms. Joanie talking back to the television. "Don't do it Nikki – Vicki, that's my girl with her crazy Cybil acting ass."

The people in the house to the left of Ms. Joanie were a religious family. The Petersons, as a family, were always on their way to church for prayer service, bible study, choir rehearsal, or something church related. They never were outside long enough to do anything but get in and out of the car. The couple never sat on the porch and the two kids never played outside in the front yard. They were pleasant enough; they spoke and kept going. The couple, Henry and Cora had two girls, Nadine and Daphine and one son who they affectionately called Tubby – he was fat. When they did play, it would be in the back yard and they could only go so far in their own yard because it led into an alley. Ms. Quincy had her doubts about these people who did not wear makeup and covered themselves from head to foot. She said God wants His children to be happy and beautiful, not dull, and lifeless. Nadine, age 16 and Daphine, age 14 were very dull and they rarely smiled. Tubby aged 17 was awkward because of his weight, so he did not come outside much at all. Gail told her mother that Mrs. Peterson made hearty meals every day. She made homemade biscuits and baked her own bread. Gail knew because one day while walking to the store she heard the mother calling to the children in the backyard to come inside because the bread was ready. The Petersons used to have a hog and a few chickens in their backyard until they ate them all. The girls were full figured, and those long robes they wore did not help their shape. When you can see their hair, it is parted down the middle in two fat braids. Mrs. Peterson does not believe in straightening or processing hair, so they are all natural. She uses the stinky Sulfur hair oil; you can smell it all the way from across the street when it is freshly done. It must work because their hair always looks strong and healthy. When caught not wearing her religious hooded frock, Mrs. Peterson had a short afro-like hair style; she looked like Florida Evans from the television show, *Good Times*.

In the house to the left of the Petersons were the Keefers. The house could be described as a shot-gun type house. You could open the front door and see all the way to the back door. You could shoot right through it and not hit a thing. The Keefers were a large family; Ollie Mae and Walter Ed had 8 children. They were the newest family on the block just moving from Coffeeville, MS. They were simple folks with grand ideas about the big city of Memphis. There were three boys and five girls. The three oldest children, John, 20, Nellgene, 19 and Edward, 17 stayed in Coffeeville with Ollie Mae's sister Bea Audrey. They had jobs and needed to stay at their school, besides Memphis was only a few hours away. They visited on weekends and holidays. Mr. Walter Ed, as everybody on the street called him, was the co-owner of a successful upholstery business in Midtown Memphis. A puny scrawny man with unusually long fingers, he worked long and hard hours. Mrs. Ollie Mae was a seamstress for a well-known uniform company in Raleigh. She was small in statue, about 5'2", but she could belt out some orders. The children feared her more than the Daddy. Jessie Faye, 14 was very smart, she told everybody she was going to be a scientist one day and discover a cure for leukemia and the common cold. Walter Ed, Jr., was 15 and he tried to keep everybody in line since he was the oldest boy of this group. Lori Ann and her fraternal twin sister Flori Ann were 13 years old. Enoch, their 9-year-old brother was the only one who could boast of being born in a real hospital. Because he had sickle cell leukemia when he was born, they were grateful that he was born in a hospital. He was the sickliest among them all going in and out of the hospital. The other children were delivered by Midwives or by their Daddy. This family was country in every sense of the word. Miss Ollie Mae did not trust banks, so she would put their earnings in a shoe box under the bed. Whenever someone needed money for school, shopping, etc., Miss Ollie Mae would go to the bedroom to retrieve the shoe box from under the bed. One day, Lori Ann needed money for a field trip; Gail was with her and when she saw Lori Ann's mother kneel, she thought she was getting ready to pray for some help. She pulled out that shoe box, opened it and inside was a small beaded purse – she pulled out a wad of bills held together by a rubber band. She did not hesitate even though Gail was standing there; I guess she figured she was a child, who would she tell.

Chapter 10

"Pick Up The Pieces" Average White Band

Gail continued to look up and down the street, hoping something exciting would happen. Lori Ann ventured across the street and asked, "Whatcha doing." Gail looked at this little girl as if she was the Messiah. She stood up stretching as tall as she could with her mouth wide open and eyes lit up. She did not say anything. Lori Ann looked at Gail in bewilderment and asked again, "Whatcha doing?" Gail answered in a cheerful way, "I'm waiting for some fun." My brother is going to the Marines to serve the country and we are having a party. The two girls looked at each other. Lori Ann Keefer was a beautiful little girl. Her skin was the color of a cast iron skillet after a good seasoning and her hair was jet black and shiny like a stallion's mane. Gail later found out that Lori Ann used a bleaching cream on her skin for lightening purposes; only Lori Ann could see the difference. Lori Ann had an oval-shaped flawless face, smooth as a baby's bottom. She hid 35% of her face with bangs. Gail thought to herself, "If I had a ruler, I bet those bangs would measure 9 or 10 inches in length. Lori Ann was tall and lean. Her clothes seemed to hang off her like bulky sweaters on a wire hanger. She had an eye for cute clothes, but she had not quite developed a fashion sense for coordinating outfits. She was wearing a red short-sleeved velour top, a red plaid pleated skirt and sandals. She had a very hesitant walk, like she was sneaking away from something. Lori Ann did not like school; she only went because everybody else her age was there.

Lori Ann told Gail that her family had just moved to the big city of Memphis from Coffeeville, Mississippi. Her whole family stayed in Coffeeville with the mother's sister in a spacious house until the Keefers decided they were crowding their relative's family of six. The young Keefer couple moved to Memphis in June of 1979, got settled, saw a steady income coming in and two years later sent for five of their eight children to relocate to Memphis from Coffeeville on North Dunbar Street.

Today, with Gail, Lori Ann decided to take the initiative when she saw her sitting outside alone. Lori Ann needed a friend and she decided Gail was going to be her friend. Gail was wearing a lime green tank top with daisies. The daisies looked like they were popping up off her shirt. She wore coordinating lime green culottes with a daisy trim. Her sandals were white with a daisy separating the first two toes. Lori Ann thought Gail seemed outgoing; she had noticed her on her porch playing a few times and thought she would be fun. She also thought she was always neat and clean. She told her mother that Gail looked like she stepped right off the pages of a store catalog. Lori Ann heard some of the neighbors say they thought the Quincy's were stuck up because they did not talk to anyone, but a few folks on the street. Some even said they thought the Quincy children were spoiled, because they always had new school clothes every year. Lori Ann wanted to fit in and have a sense of belonging, so she knew Gail would be her best choice. When Lori Ann came up, it was a welcome surprise. Gail thought Lori Ann would be a good friend to have just across the street. They did not realize that they both needed each other.

The girls became inseparable. All summer long, they played together every day. They were at each other's houses, playing jacks on the porch, playing kickball in the backyard, playing dress up in their mother's closets, playing with Barbie dolls, doing puzzles, etc. They even started wearing each other's clothes, much to Gail's mother chagrin. "If you don't have it, wear something else," she shouted, once she noticed Gail wearing Lori Ann's rainbow-colored shirt. Gail whined so about it being fun to swap clothes that her mother gave in and let them continue. They had slumber parties together. Gail had the most fun at Lori Ann's and Lori Ann had the most fun at Gail's. Gail loved Lori Ann's mother because every time she came over for a sleepover, she would buy all kinds of junk food: soda, cheeseburgers, potato chips, hot dogs, windmill cookies, stage planks, ice cream sandwiches and lots of chocolate. She would also let them stay up until the television went off, generally on Fridays at midnight. They both loved scary movies so they would watch the double feature for Friday night while eating all their snacks. They would stay up even longer than midnight just talking or looking through magazines. Lori Ann loved Gail's mother because she would play board games with them, show them how to cook and help them make up their own fun games. All the sisters and brothers were cordial to each other, but Gail and Lori Ann had a *true-blue* friendship.

One night while at Lori Ann's for a sleepover, Gail decided she wanted to measure Lori Ann's bangs. Lori Ann's Mom sewed, so Gail asked her if she could borrow her measuring tape. Gail skipped back to Lori Ann's room. Lori Ann was taking her clothes off so she could put on her PJ's. She was not modest in the least about her body. She took off her bra and panties and slipped on a cute purple pajama short set. In was mid-July, so it was hotter than hot outside. Lori Ann's room was cool and comfortable. Gail stood in the doorway flabbergasted at such freedom. Lori Ann looked at her and said, "We have the same thing and my brothers never come back here." Lori Ann's room was at the very back of the house. It used to be a back porch, but her father put up walls, added electrical outlets and light fixtures; it was a genuinely nice room, complete with a bathroom. "Go ahead and put on your PJ's so we can watch this movie." Gail grabbed her clothes and toothbrush and walked quietly towards the bathroom. Lori Ann blasted in a southern drawl that came out every now and then, "What you got so special?" Gail said, "I just don't want to change my clothes in the open like you." Lori Ann did not have doors that lead to her room, but she had some cool multi-colored beads for the entrance. They looked like candy streaming down from the top to bottom. When Gail walked through the beads back into the bedroom, Lori Ann said, "You're a weird girl." Gail walked back and forth through the beads and then popped her head back through halfway saying, "It takes a weird one to know a weird one, so you are a weird one, too." They both laughed uncontrollably and wound up on the floor. Lori Ann seriously asked Gail was she going to forget about her when school started. "Are you going to be my friend when school starts?" Gail stood up and said, "For real? Best friends never forget each other – For real!" They hugged and said, "Yay," Gail started to measure Lori Ann's bangs and then they said, "the movie!" they both shouted, realizing they were missing the best part, the beginning.

Chapter 11

"Jesus is on the Main line, tell him what you want – call Him up and tell Him what you want…"
The Brown Sisters

The best thing about sleeping over at each other's houses was the fact that they got to walk to church together. They went to Sunday school and stayed for service. The church was just around the corner, so they enjoyed walking together. Gail's sisters would join them, but most of the time they walked ahead or behind to be by themselves. Gail's mother encouraged Lori Ann to come to church for a visit and she eventually joined. The church, Believers Missionary Baptist Church was a small white wooden building on the corner. It was quite an impressive building with a steeple on top bearing a stained-glass cross with a golden center. The membership on the role was about 400, but the attendance every Sunday was probably about 200, so it was a nice crowd. Everybody knew everybody. There were some prominent families in the congregation, and they tended to try and run the church whenever they got the chance. When adding a Life Center, they wanted to have the final say on the design and when starting a nursery for the neighborhood; they let their objections be known. "We don't want Bae-Bae's kids running around in our church." They were often unsuccessful; they stayed because their parents grew up in the church or because they were baptized there. They all had special seats where they liked to sit, and God forbid a visitor come in and sit beside them – you would think you were at the North Pole. The preacher, Rev. Lee David Phillips was a sweet elderly gentleman, who loved the Lord and his entire congregation. Every time the choir sang, or somebody made a speech, he would say after the 1ˢᵗ applause, "Give them another hand." He had a kind and gentle disposition which put everyone at ease. He prided himself on getting to know everyone and making them feel special by remembering their names, their spouses, children, occupations, etc. He took a genuine interest in his members and they appreciated his personal demeanor. He was like the grandfather you wished you had in your family.

Gail and Lori Ann were happy to be in the same Sunday school class, youth ages 10 – 14. Their teacher, Ms. Venora Cromwell appeared as though she was 70 years old, but we later found out she was only 57 years old. She had blue-gray short curly hair and she always wore a handkerchief-type doily-looking cloth on her head. Her small framed glasses were always perched on her nose and they had a dangling chain on them for when she took her glasses off and they hung like a necklace around her neck. She was a medium brown skinny lady who had a smell like a bowl of peppermints that were sitting in the sun and they all stuck together. She always dressed in layers; she would have on a nice suit with a sweater and then a shawl over that; she would wear thick flesh colored support hose with comfortable orthopedic shoes. When she sat down, you could see where she put the hose in knots near her knee to keep them up. She always looked disheveled and she always rushed us through the lesson. "Stand up Quincy and hurry up and read the key verse," she would say in a raspy voice. She would make the whole class read it together until it met with her satisfaction. She would not stand for any disrespect or unruliness in her class – she would "put you in your place." She would read the lesson under her breath in a mumbling manner and then she would look up and say, "Do you have your Sunday school offering." Gail and Lori Ann always put 2 quarters in for offering. Lori Ann liked to throw Ms. Cromwell for a loop by asking a philosophical or theoretical question about the lesson. "Why didn't Jonah just stick a sword in the whale's mouth to get out or light a fire or something?" Ms. Cromwell would simply ignore Lori Ann's question by pretending she did not hear her and say, "Let us all read the closing prayer and head to the sanctuary."

For service, Gail and Lori Ann always sat in the balcony. There, they could sneak candy, chew gum and pass notes. There were 2 ushers on duty, but they were always asleep at their post. Most teens and 20 – 25-year-old folks sat upstairs. Lori Ann said, "I guess they had not decided to become one of them yet – the downstairs church folk." During the announcement segment, Mrs. Conner, who had been making the announcements since forever, would always get up quickly and rush to the podium as if she were on her way to somewhere else. She was a petite-sized woman, mid-50s, her hair was dyed a cognac burnt orange color and she would wear loud colors like orange, fuchsia or yellow – even in the wintertime, seemingly to match her hair. During the announcements, she would always say, pacific instead of specific when reminding the young people about upcoming events. "I need you to listen quietly to the *pacific* dates so you will be on time and be ready," she said. Lori Ann didn't realize some of the errors until Gail pointed them out to her. She would also add s to men and women; we really squirmed then. "The *mens* and *womens* of the church are having a fundraiser and we would like the young people to attend as well." The bad part was that she was an elementary school teacher, and nobody ever corrected her. Maybe she only said boys and girls and talked only about the Pacific Ocean. She was funny, but we would never laugh in her face or be disrespectful. Besides, those faux pas, she was quite intelligent.

"Girl look at Ms. Conner today," Lori Ann whispered. She is wearing that yellow suit again. "She looks like sunshine walking up to the podium on this cloudy day." "Shhh, I want to hear what she has to say," Gail insisted. Gail liked to listen to speeches, announcements, and presentations; she also liked reading the program and any other printed material; she was always trying to catch grammar or spelling errors. She corrected Lori Ann all the time, but Lori Ann just blew her off and did not take it seriously. One day, Lori Ann said, "I fin to go find me something to wear to church in the morning." Gail said, "You're about to or you're going to, but you're not *fin* to do anything." Lori Ann would get Gail back by talking about some outfit she had on that she had worn more than once during the last two weeks. "You're going to wear the dog and puppy out of that, ain't you?" Gail hated when she used colloquialisms, but oftentimes found herself sayings some of the same phrases later as they became closer. "I thought I saw a *hank* last night walking past my bedroom door," Gail told Lori Ann one day. "Don't you mean a ghost or a spirit, MissyMae?" Lori Ann would muse. "Well, I was just saying *hank* because I knew you would immediately know what I was talking about," she said with a smile. "Why would a ghost be visiting your house? It was brand new when y'all moved in it," Lori Ann said. "Maybe we're disturbing a grave site, or somebody is coming back to tell us something," Gail said. "Whoooo-whaaaat – you watch too many scary movies," Lori Ann said while motioning her arms up and down. Gail slumped down on the floor and covered her eyes while Lori Ann was making fun of her. "I knew you were going to make fun of me if I told you. I really did see something."

Chapter 12

"The Hustle" Van McCoy and The Soul City Symphony

On a cool September afternoon, a week before school was to start, Gail and Lori Ann were sitting on the front steps of Lori Ann's house watching people and cars pass. "That's my car – a green Monte Carlo," said Lori Ann. "I wonder what Nadine is going to get from the store," said Gail. "She'll definitely bring back some cookies," grinned Lori Ann. "1, 2, 3, good luck for me I see a yellow cab," said Gail. The cab pulled in front of Gail's house and the girls stood up at the same time. "I never heard of that before," Lori Ann whispered because she could tell Gail was focused on that cab. Gail waved her hand to silence Lori Ann as she began to walk down the steps towards her house for a better view. The cab door opened and out stood a tall, handsome man dressed in a green camouflage uniform. As the man went to the trunk to pull out a long green duffle bag, she could see from the profile that it was her brother, Aldwin. He was back from the Marines; Gail ran across the street to greet him. Lori Ann followed out of curiosity. She did not really know Gail's brother because he left the day the girls met. Of course, she knew he was in the Marines because every time Aldwin wrote a letter or sent a postcard, Gail would bring it over to Lori Ann's house for all to see.

"Who is this tall, dark and handsome military man?" Gail said as she tip-toed across the street towards Aldwin. Aldwin turned around and looked over Gail's head. "I hear my baby sister, but I don't see her – where is she?" Aldwin pretended not to see Gail until she started pulling on his jacket. "It's me, right here, I know you see me – I'm going to tell Momma," Gail whined. "Oh, if I hadn't heard that whining voice coming out of you, I would have never thought this was my little baby sister. You certainly have grown up for the last few months I've been away – who is your little friend?" Gail, tired from trying to get Aldwin's attention, said with fast breathing, "This is my across the street friend, Lori Ann." "Hello across the street friend, Lori Ann, he repeated. Lori Ann was very shy around everybody except Gail, so she tried to hide under her bangs. "Hi." Aldwin could barely hear her and he bent down close thinking she was going to say something else. "Watch out," he told them, "I think I heard a mouse." They both jumped around like kernels in a hot pot of oil about to pop. Aldwin threw the duffle bag over his shoulder, laughed, and headed towards the house. Gail and Lori Ann looked at each other and realized the joke was on them.

Ms. Quincy came out on the porch to see who got out of the cab or who called a cab. When she saw that it was Aldwin, she ran towards him laughing and crying at the same time. They had the longest embrace and walked arm and arm inside. "You must have known I was cooking your favorites today; neckbones, cabbage, mashed potatoes and an apple carrot raisin salad. This is a wonderful surprise! Gail and Lori Ann jumped off the porch and walked backed across the street.

During the summer, their mother would spend $100 on each child for school supplies, school clothes, shoes, and other incidentals. She would usually get the oldest child's things first and work her way down. It would take at least six pay periods to get everything. Sometimes she would put things in the lay-a-way, but she preferred to pay for it all at once, because the younger kids didn't understand the concept of picking something and not being able to take it home with you that day. Their mother would often order many of their school clothes from the Sears catalog. She would let them circle the things they liked, and she would go back and choose four or five of the outfits. It would always be a big presentation and she would lay the new clothes on their beds and when they came in from playing. They would see the new things and scream with excitement. They would immediately want to try them on, and everybody would model their new outfits. It would be like a mini fashion show, complete with music and narration. From the "fashion show," their mother would determine what socks, barrettes, etc. would be needed to accessorize the outfits. Their mother would be the Mistress of Ceremonies and she would give vivid descriptions of each outfit from the pearl buttons on their sweaters to the hound's-tooth pattern of their skirts. She watched her soap operas or stories as she would call them; she watched *As the World Turns* and *The Edge of Night*. They had great fashions on the stories, she would say many times "look at how Monica is dressed today; she is sharp as a tack." She also read Ebony, Jet, Good Housekeeping, and McCall's magazines religiously. She loved looking at the fashions in all the magazines and trying to duplicate some of the styles. She didn't think you had to spend hundreds of dollars to have a stylist outfit. Her children were always clean and smartly dressed for school and church. Their mother would always say, "We may not have a lot, but what we have will be clean and pressed."

They walked to high school together and when Lori Ann got a car, she picked up Gail every day. She even picked her up from cheerleader practice and from some of the home games. Gail thrived in school and Lori Ann had some challenges keeping up. They remained close friends and continued to have sleepovers on the weekends. Lori Ann was known for being the best-dressed in school and Gail was known for being more studious. Gail was making new friends and making new strides as a budding adult while Lori Ann was still apprehensive when it came to meeting new people. Gail was on her way to earning a four-year college scholarship where she would major in English. Lori Ann was certain she could get in the local community college to pursue a Fashion Merchandising degree.

They were both happy that they decided to stay in the city for college. Once they started at their respective colleges, they compared notes almost daily, but those comparisons became few and far between as the semesters rolled along.

Chapter 13

"Sweet dreams are made of this, who am I to disagree..." Eurythmics

8 years later since middle school I've seen this - "This is it," Gail whispered to herself, as she read the flyer posted on the college's student union bulletin board:

Zeta Xi Zeta Sorority
Rush Party
Thursday, March 3rd, 4:30 p.m.
Room 206 Doris Shaw Student Center
Business Casual attire preferred

Gail thought to herself, "What is business casual?" She further thought, "my favorite middle school teacher is a Zeta, two of my Sunday School teachers are Zetas, my favorite English professor is a Zeta. I want to be a Zeta!" Gail was not quite sure what being a Zeta was all about, but she wanted to learn more about it. This was her opportunity to finally meet the ladies of Zeta; she had seen them on campus doing various activities and programs. Their reputation on campus was that they were very friendly, real smart, great steppers and community service driven. The Zetas always had the highest-grade point average on campus among other Greek-letter organizations. Because it was just Monday, Gail felt she had plenty of time to get ready for Thursday's Rush Party. She wanted to impress the ladies, but she also wanted the ladies to impress her. As a Freshman, her plans were to attend all the Rush parties of all the sororities and make up her mind which one best represented a group she wanted to be affiliated with the rest of her life. Gail called Lori Ann and told her all about it. "Are you listening to me?" Lori Ann was not interested in college or sorority life. Because she tried it for 1 semester and failed miserably, she really was not trying to hear Gail's story. Lori Ann realized she had coasted through high school and was totally unprepared for college, socially or academically. "They are the smartest on campus and they are always doing some type of community service...and you know my favorite colors are blue and orange," Gail continued. "Go for it, then," Lori Ann piped in quickly trying to be enthusiastic for Gail, all the while hoping they could move on to another subject. "Okay, I will." Gail ended the discussion after finally getting Lori Ann's approval. "Are we going to the Naval Base Thursday night?" Lori Ann asked. "That is the same day as Zeta's Rush Party, let's wait and see. I might have to do something with them. I'll let you know, okay?" Lori Ann quickly said, "Okay, but let me know so I can make other plans; I can always go with Lynn. She loves to go." Gail paused for a second, made a smirky face and said, "okay." Gail and Lynn did not get along. Lynn was like 26 and still trying to hang with them and go to clubs. She had a job and 2 children. Gail thought she should be home with her children, helping them with their homework or baking cakes or something. "I don't know why you don't like Lynn," Lori Ann said. "She's really cool even though she does get on my nerve with all that fake talking. Lynn liked to pretend she was not from Memphis by talking in a Northern high-pitched tone. It was very annoying to Gail and to Lori Ann., but they tolerated her because she could talk her way out of anything and into everything. Gail pretended to be Lynn – "Memphis is a quiet little Southern town; I love downtown. Have you been there, downtown?" Lori Ann responded pretending to be Lynn – "Memphis is gorgeous darling, but I must say Beale

Street is simply the best kept secret around." They both laughed. Lori Ann asked Gail, "Have you told your family about the Rush party yet?" Lori Ann asked Gail that because she knew her sisters had argued about it earlier. "No," Gail said. "I'm just going to wait and see how it all goes first." Alex and Angela really gave her a hard time about it. They told her, she had 3 sisters, why does she need more? They called sororities cults and said she would probably get beat with a paddle. They wondered why you must get humiliated to join; they heard about Greek-lettered organizations from friends, but none had experienced it on campus. Adrianne went to college for two years; she wanted to be a veterinarian, but had to drop out when she met Gaston, her husband. They had three children, so all of that was put on an indefinite hold. Adrianne was never a joiner. In fact, she always stayed to herself and was never very social. She was always pleasant, but she did not care to be around anyone other than her family. She had 3 friends throughout high school, and she could take them or leave them. Angela, on the other hand, was extremely popular in high school. Everybody loved her and wanted to be around her. She went on to a private college and got a bachelor's degree in Management. She did not keep in touch with her high school friends and was not very social during her college years. She went to class and came home. She graduated and did not look back.

Chapter 14

"Oh Mickey, what a pity you don't understand. You take me by the heart when you take me by the hand..." Toni Basil

Gail's mother was her biggest fan and supporter. She came to all the games in middle school and high school to watch her cheer. She came to all the Honor Society programs, Glee Club concerts and gave her input when Gail was Editor of yearbook and newspaper. Whatever books were assigned in college, Gail's Mom would read them too, so they could discuss them. This would help Gail tremendously in the classroom for discussions, research papers or presentations. Gail's Mom never discouraged her from doing anything educational, social, and positive.

"What are you all dressed up for," Gail's mother said while grabbing Gail's arm and twirling her around. Gail was wearing a white lace-collared blouse, a black skirt with white polka-dots and black loafers. "There's a program today at 4:30, Gail said. Her mother spoke up, "You did not tell me about a program; what kind of program?" her mother asked. Gail's mother loved going to campus for speakers, concerts, lectures, and workshops. "It is a sorority Rush party, "Gail said slowly. "Which one is it," her mother asked. "Zeta Xi Zeta," Gail excitedly said. She could not contain her enthusiasm anymore. Today was the day and she wanted the world to know how anxious she was about this organization. "Oh, Zeta, yes, that's a fine group," Gail's mother said. "They hosted that political forum we went to a couple of months ago. I hear it is pretty expensive to join, though." Gail had heard that joining a sorority could be expensive, so she started saving $50 from her monthly school work study checks last Fall. She saved $300. "I saved some money from my work study job and I am hoping if I get accepted, I can get a part-time job and get the rest needed." Her mother said, "Well, you know I'll help out in any way I can. You do not need to do anything but concentrate on school and getting good grades. If it's something you really want to do." Gail went over to her mother and kissed her on the cheek and gave her a big hug. "I really want this," Gail said. "I got to leave now, so I won't miss the bus; I have to be on time for this event. I will see you later." Gail's mother yelled as Gail ran towards the front door, "Gail, good luck and call me if you need me to pick you up. You know I don't like you at the bus stop too late."

Umbrellas, cups, bracelets, jackets, books, shirts, caps and even socks – Gail never saw so much stuff adorned with the Zeta Xi Zeta Greek letters. The room where the Rush Party was held was decked out in blue streamers, orange balloons and festive posters. One table was full of framed pictures, scrapbooks, figurines, and photo albums. Gail leafed through the albums and noticed a few familiar faces from campus. She did not realize the organization was so large. "Welcome to our Rush Party, my name is Peggy, I've seen you on campus, is your name Gail?" The voice came from a tall, gorgeous woman who could pass for a young Dionne Warwick. "Yes, my name is April Gail Quincy." Gail was extremely nervous, but she did not want to seem that way, so what does she do when she is nervous? Talk…and talk. "My friends and family call me Gail, that's my middle name. I know three Zetas and I can't wait to hear more about your organization; I love the colors, too. Blue and Orange is really cute together." Before Gail could say anything else, Peggy jumped in and said, "Okay, Gail, that's great, please sign in over there and find a seat because we're going to start in just a few minutes." Gail walked over to the sign-in table thinking how stupid and immature she must have sounded to Peggy. As she was writing her name, she heard someone say, "Gail, is that April Gail." Gail did not have to turn around, the only person that called her April Gail was her 6th grade teacher, Mrs. T.S. Dotson. Gail bounced when turning around with a big smile. "Hi Mrs. Dotson," Gail said with a cheerleader exuberance. Mrs. Dotson was wearing a blue Zeta oxford button-down shirt and a blue pleated skirt. To Gail, Mrs. Dotson looked exactly the same as when she was in her class. "Hey Baby, you know the best sorority, don't you?" Gail robotically responded, "Yes Mrs. Dotson. She remembered that in Mrs. Dotson's class, there was no, yes, uh-huh, etc., you had to say Yes Mrs. Dotson or No Mrs. Dotson. "Everybody, this is my baby, April Gail Quincy. She was one of the best students in my 6th and 7th grade English classes." "You don't have to tell us who she is said another familiar voice." We see her every Sunday holding her post at church. She's a good Usher" It was two or her church members, Ms. Earline Caster and Mrs. Dottie Buckley. Both gave her welcoming hugs and nods of approval. Gail was happy to see the familiar faces and to get the attention.

Gail was thinking to herself; this is the most wonderful moment of embarrassment she had ever experienced. Peggy stood up from the head table and motioned to several Zetas in the back that they were ready to get started. Mrs. Dotson told Gail to sit in the front so she could hear everything. Gail headed up to the front and Mrs. Dotson made her stop by the display table so she could take her picture. She took lots of pictures of the classes in middle school; she always had a camera, and this was no exception. Peggy began, "Welcome to the 1983 Spring Rush Party, "the other Zetas said altogether, "We're happy you're here!" After the program, Mrs. Dotson, Mrs. Caster and Mrs. Buckley handed Gail an envelope. They all had their hands on it like sports players in a huddle about to say, "Go Team." Mrs. Dotson said, "open it later and let us know if you need more. When Gail got on the bus to go home, she read through all the material they gave her about the organization. She was impressed with all the things the sorority was doing – walking for babies, entertaining kids at shelters, partnering with corporations to give job readiness training, working with elected officials, volunteering at call centers, digging wells in Africa, registering new voters, collecting eyeglasses, etc. Gail came across the envelope that the ladies had given her – she brought it close to her heart and opened it slowly. It was 3 $100 bills with a note paper clipped to them: Every year we come to the Rush Party in hopes of finding that one young lady who outshines the group – you were the one. We want to help continue the tradition of our Founders by offering this financial assistance. Please let us know if you need anything else. Congratulations – we look forward to calling you "Sister." It was signed the The Triumphant Three, Spring 1963. Gail was overcome with emotion and tears began to roll down her cheeks. She was so distracted that the bus driver had been sitting at her stop for a few seconds before she realized this was her stop. She thanked him and hurried off the bus. She ran all the way home; she was excited to tell her mother all about the Rush Party, the great things about the sorority and the wonderful gift she received from her future "sisters."

Chapter 15

"Take your passion and make it happen..." Irene Cara

Three weeks later, Gail wondered how much longer she would have to participate in the pledging process. She barely had time to do homework, hang out with her friends and do her chores around the house. Her mother asked her several times when she was going to do her laundry because her hamper was overflowing. The Big Sisters always had them doing something. Because she did not live on campus and did not have a car, she had to depend on her sisters. One evening the "line" of 12 went to the Veteran's hospital to play Bingo with the men on the 8th floor. Another morning, they were reading to kids at a daycare and one night they helped a candidate for City Council fold and mail brochures. At least three days a week they were busy, but what she liked most was having game night with the ladies of the sorority. They got to play board games, charades, and cards. It did not matter that they had to serve snacks to each Big Sister. This event occurred every Friday and it was always fun seeing all the sisters together. This Friday, they were told to bring a royal blue dress because they were going to take some pictures. So, in addition to loading up the car with games, Gail also had to put her dress in plastic, pack her hose, shoes, accessories, etc. She knew this was going to be a long and busy night. The line of ladies arrived in the parking lot of the University Center; some drove, and some walked over from their dorms. Everybody was assigned to do something: bring paper products, bring beverages, etc. No one went into the University Center until all 12 were there and had their designated items. They lined up, items in tow, and headed to the game room on the 1ˢᵗ floor. They had to pass the computer lab and the coffee shop to get to the game room. It was the largest room at the very end of the hall. It had an arcade side with PacMan, Galaxy and Centipede. It also had a few pool, ping pong and air hockey tables. The area where they set up had tables, couches, and loveseats. It was like a small living room decorated with the school's colors; lamps, throw rugs and pillows added just the right home touch. Gail thought maybe she could stay on campus for her last year if they could afford it. Her mother did not think it made sense for her to pay extra money to live on campus when she was only a few miles away from the campus. The line of ladies headed towards the long table in the back near the kitchen to put the items down before preparation.

"Put your stuff down and change into your blue dress," one of the big sisters said sharply. Some headed towards the kitchen to put cold items in the refrigerator and Gail put the games on the table. Gail started to get her garment bag which was draped over one of the chairs when she heard, "Hurry Up!" They scurried into the meeting room's restroom. Luckily, it had a mirrored room for changing separate from the toilet area. When everyone had all buttons buttoned, sashes tied, zippers zipped and straps strapped, they lined up in order of height and walked slowly, but ever so gracefully down the hall to the game room. One of the big sisters stopped them at the door, "I love this sea of blue, but let me check you out to make sure you look presentable – I don't want you messing up the picture." She walked up and down the line like a drill sergeant, "tighten up that belt, tuck in that bra strap, pull that slip up," she ordered. Once they all got approval, they were told to meet the other big sisters in the private dining hall on the 2ⁿᵈ floor for pictures. They could not all fit in the elevator comfortably, so they headed to the stairs and clunked up the one flight. The new heels on their shoes made loud noises on the concrete stairwell steps – they sounded like a bunch of horses trotting upstairs.

When they got to the private dining hall, the room was beautifully decorated in royal blue and orange. The dining room was very impressive with oak furniture and tiffany lighting. This is where Greek Advisors had retreats and the Dean of Students met with her Executive Board. There were current pictures of each registered student organization on the walls. Gail did not recognize some of the clubs like Gaming Club, Future Lawyers of America, Total Wellness Group, Social Worker's United, and Memphis Geeks Society. Many were self explanatory, but the Gaming Club was misleading, because it featured students who were interested in playing board games like Scrabble, Monopoly, Clue, etc.

There was a huge banner on the front wall of the room, with "Welcome Spring Line." Gail smelled all kinds of food and saw a table adored with a buffet of dishes, but she could not think about food right now. There was another sight she wanted to get a closer look at that was along the back wall. There were 12 jacket-covered chairs in" line" order. Each blue jacket had the orange Greek letters on the right, the sister's first name on the front in script and the given "line" names on the back. Gail's jacket had *Sunshine* on the back; she liked it and could not wait to put it on. In each chair was a beautifully decorated basket filled with goodies: shirts, cups, buttons, stationery, jewelry, key chains, and photo frames. The Big sisters swarmed around them like they were pageant winners and started explaining the chosen line names. They gave them the secret handshake, did the infamous sorority call – *Hmmm Yeah* - and made sure each new member had their membership certificate, chapter key and a guidebook. The President began to speak, "Ladies! Congratulations! My new sisters, are you ready to continue the tradition and work hard for the sisterhood?" They all screamed, "Yes!" She asked them to raise their right hand and take a pledge of dedication. Afterwards, she asked the other sisters to raise their left hands and take a pledge of re-dedication. It was April 1, 1983; Gail kept hoping this was not an April Fool's joke. The mascot is a hummingbird, so all you saw were wings flapping and all you could hear was, *Hmmm Yeah!* Once all the commotion settled and they took their last picture altogether, the President lead them, out of order, towards the buffet table. Among the various dishes were little bouquets of blue and orange flowers. It was a beautiful spread! They used a cookbook that had famous sorority members' recipes. She saw a dish by her favorite teacher, Mrs. Dotson. *Sister Thelma Dotson's Spinach Lasagna, Sister Earline Casters' Deviled Eggs, Sister Dottie Buckley's 3-Bean Salad, Sister Flora Calloway's chicken salad, Sister Susan Brady's ambrosia, Sister Rochelle Gates' Swedish meatballs* and the table was adorned with many more dishes: savory, sweet and scrumptious! Just as they were settled down and about to eat, members of the sponsoring chapter came in singing the sorority song and bearing gifts. Gail was happy to see Mrs. Dotson and her church members. The crying and picture taking started all over again. They partied until midnight and Gail got dropped off by one of her sisters! When she got on her porch and opened the door, she was floating on happiness, like a hummingbird! She woke up her mother to tell her she made it and her mother said, "Good, I'm very happy for you - now go to bed before you wake up the whole house." Who could sleep – "I am a member of Zeta Xi Zeta Sorority" Gail screamed, "Hmmm Yeah! ""April Gail Quincy," her Mom bellowed. "Yes ma'am, I am going to bed. Goodnight - I love you."

Chapter 16

"My name is Luka, I live on the second floor…"
Susan Vega

Her name was Denise Renee Thomas, they called her Nee-Nee, she was 10 years old, the only daughter of the young couple who moved next door to Gail in the early part of the Summer. She just sat on the porch and played jacks. When Gail walked by on her way to or from the store, she would speak to her saying "Hello Neighbor." They had been there about two months and Gail still didn't know their names. One day Gail walked by and said,, "I sure would like to know my new neighbor's name." Denise whispered, "Nee-Nee." Gail said, "I can't hear you." Denise shouted, "NEE-NEE!" Suddenly, a thirty something thin-framed coffee brown woman comes out the door letting the screen door slam behind her. "What's all the screaming about?" she looks down at her daughter. Nee-Nee looks up and says, "Momma, I was just telling our neighbor my name." Gail chimed in quietly, "Hi my name is April Quincy and I was trying to get to know my new neighbor. The mother barked out with, "Her name is Denise and my name is Rhonda Thomas. My husband's name is Dwayne. We adopted Denise Renee when she was just three months old." Gail was shocked that Ms. Thomas was so forthcoming with information. Nee-Nee did not seem fazed by the conversation at all. Nee-Nee appeared awkward as she listened to her mother go on and on about the adoption. As her mother talked about how the birth mother was only 16 and was a distant relative of hers from Chicago, Nee-Nee began to withdraw into the darkest corner of the porch behind the wrought iron swing. "We just love our little Nee-Nee; people say she looks like me." When they noticed Nee-Nee was not around, they started to look for her. Suddenly, Mr. Thomas comes to the screen door. "What's all this jaw japing about – get in this house both of you, it is almost supper time." Ms. Thomas in almost a whisper said, "I was just telling our neighbor, April, about Nee-Nee and us." Gail waved hello and said, "call me Gail." Mr. Thomas said, "Well, nice to meet you, we're going in now to eat supper." Before Gail could say nice to meet you too, the door was closed.

At least three days of the week, Nee-Nee would go to Gail's house and sit. She would watch television with Gail, walk to the store with Gail or help Gail with her chores. She especially liked to hang clothes with Gail; Nee-Nee liked trying to hide behind the sheets and towels. Nee-Nee told Gail that when she went to college, she was going to join Zeta Xi Zeta so she could be her sister. Gail told her she was already like a little sister to her. Nee-Nee's mother was a records clerk at the public library and her Dad was a probation officer. He always boasted that he was proud to be keeping the city safe. Nee-Nee told Gail one day, "My Daddy says being a probation officer is the best job ever, but I think I would like to see different folks once and a while without a criminal record." Because her Mom and Dad worked odd hours, they did not mind Nee-Nee hanging out next door. Ms. Thomas told Nee-Nee, "Gail is a sweet girl, she's not fast or anything; I don't mind you going over there from time to time. Just don't wear your welcome out."

One day while Gail was playing hopscotch with Nee-Nee, she could hear Mr. Thomas ask his wife while they were swinging along on the porch, "What could they possibly have in common? She's so much older than Nee-Nee." Ms. Thomas said, "They have fun together and Gail is a good influence on Nee-Nee. She is smart and has good manners. She wants to finish her college degree, teach English and be a writer." He began to stand up when he noticed some boys trying to use his yard as a shortcut. "Get out of my yard; this ain't no shortcut for y'all." He turned towards Ms. Thomas, "They going to ruin my grass and have that path bald from tracking through it. I can already see a dent in that area." "You scared them enough hollering; I am sure they will not be back through here," Ms. Thomas said. "Where did the girls go?" Mr. Thomas bellowed. Ms. Thomas pointed, "There they are right across the street sitting on the steps with another little girl. I don't think I have met her."

"I hope the pictures Aldwin took of us come out nice," said Gail while sitting on Lori's Ann's steps. "Ever since he got that camera, he has been taking pictures of everything and anything," Lori Ann added. "That was his hobby while he was in the military and he is really good at it, said Gail, taking up for her big brother. Nee-Nee was happy to be hanging with big girls, so she did not say much; she did not want them teasing her. "A yellow cab," she screamed. They all said, "1,2,3, good luck for me, I see a yellow cab. Nee-Nee stood up to try and catch a lightning bug. "The bugs are out, so it will soon be time to go in," Gail said. Lori Ann pulled Gail closer to her and whispered, "You got to catch me up on your college gossip and tell me what Zeta Xi Zeta's next big event will be for the end of the semester."

Mr. Thomas said, "Mosquitoes are starting to bite; I am going in, are you coming?" Pulling her legs up around her, Mrs. Thomas said, "No, I'm going to sit out a little while longer and enjoy the cool breeze." "Rhonda, keep an eye on the girls," Mr. Thomas said as he opened the screen door. As it slammed behind him, you could hear him mumbling something about girls and boys being outside sniffing each other like dogs. Ms. Thomas rocked slowly as she watched the kids racing in the street. They had just got a good game of red light/green light when the streetlights popped on. Everybody knew their mothers would be calling soon for them to come inside, so they hemmed and hawed towards their various destinations on the street. Gail saw her sisters in her driveway, so she waved goodbye to everybody and headed home. Nee-Nee ran across the street into her mother's open arms and they went inside happily with their arms locked together. Gail's mother was on the porch watering her plants; but Adrienne, Alex and Gail were in the driveway talking about the good old days playing in the street and rushing home when the streetlights came on. "We were like roaching running from the light," Alex said "Did y'all have a good time outside like old times?" their mother asked. They all said, "Yes ma'am." "Good, but just like old times, y'all smell like outside, come on in and get some dinner."

School had finally started after a long hot summer. This was the 2nd week and Momma was sitting on the porch waiting to see the kids walking home. Nee-Nee ran up to the porch and sat next to her. "I'm waiting on Gail," she said. "That's fine, but shouldn't you let your folks know you made it home, first. I saw your Dad pull into the driveway about an hour ago." Nee-Nee hesitated, "Okay, but tell Gail I will be back." Gail made the college track team, so she did not get home until 5:30. Nee-Nee greeted her in the driveway, but Gail was too tired from her first day of practice. She told Nee-Nee she was going to eat, shower and go to bed. Nee-Nee asked, "Can I help you study or call out some literary words?" "Naw, I got to write a 2-page essay on a question from one of the books we're reading in English and I have some History homework to concentrate on tonight. I'll see you later." Nee-Nee hung her head down and slowly walked down the driveway and into her yard across the grass to the porch. Gail had not seen Nee-Nee's mother in a while and wondered if she got a new job or something. Maybe that was why Nee-Nee seemed so needy and lonely lately.

One morning Nee-Nee went over to Gail's house early before school. She wanted to walk instead of her Dad driving her. Because her Dad drove her, she often left later while everyone else was walking. Gail was headed towards the bus stop and did not have time to chat. Gail waved good bye and said, "Pay attention and be good in school today." Before Nee-Nee could respond, her Dad shouted, "Nee-Nee come on over here." He was standing on the porch wearing a white t-shirt and what looked like pajama bottoms.

"I'm going to walk today," Nee-Nee said. Mr. Thomas came off the porch through his yard and to the end of the bushes that separated the yard. He peeked his head around the bush and said, "Nee-Nee c'mon." Tears began to well up in her eyes. "I'll see y'all after school – Bye," Nee-Nee said sorrowfully. Gail continued to walk off, but as she looked behind her, she could see Mr. Thomas grab Nee-Nee around her neck and playfully, but forcibly pushed her towards the house. Gail wondered, "what's the big deal with Nee-Nee wanting to walk to school."

When Gail came home from track practice, she noticed lots of cars at the Thomas house. She also noticed immediately that Nee-Nee was not there to greet her. "Oh well," she thought, maybe they are having company and she cannot come outside. Gail did not ever admit it, but she loved all the attention that Nee-Nee gave her. Even though she was in college, she loved coming home to "play" with Nee-Nee. Then there were times when she just did not want to be bothered with the little girl for various reasons. Many times, she would send Nee-Nee home because she grew tired of her hovering over her and hanging on her every word. Most times, though, she loved playing jacks with her, and she especially loved making paper dolls. Gail would make the people and Nee-Nee would design the outfits. They would make enough clothes for each season and then color them. They would always make a family: husband, wife and 3 children. Nee-Nee thought Gail's 64-box of crayon had every color in the world in it and she would press down hard on the crayons just so she could use the crayon sharpener on the back of the box. When Gail gave Nee-Nee the box of crayons before school started, she gave Gail the biggest hug. While hugging her neck tightly, Nee-Nee whispered, "I will never forget you." Gail walked into the house and everybody was sitting in the living room incredibly quiet. "What's the matter, did somebody die or something?"

Gail's mother explained that Nee-Nee complained of being sick while at school. The school nurse gave Nee-Nee a thorough examination after she told her that her private area was hurting. The nurse called a social worker who came in and talked to Nee-Nee for an hour. The social worker called the principal and the principal called the police and Ms. Thomas. It seemed that Mr. Thomas had been having sex with Nee-Nee almost every morning for the last year. Because Ms. Thomas refused to believe the allegations, she did not press charges against her husband, Nee-Nee had to be removed from the home and placed in foster care. "Ms. Thomas is in complete denial and does not believe her husband would do such a horrible thing – she told the social worker that Nee-Nee probably made it all up." Gail said, "You can't make up that kind of story." The social worker will be by later to collect some of Nee-Nee's things and she will not return to school. Gail was in shock as her Mom told her all the events and gruesome stories of how Mr. Thomas used to abuse Nee-Nee almost every morning before school. The police interviewed neighbors to ask if they noticed any abnormal behavior. Gail's mother just said that Mr. Thomas seemed overprotective but what father wasn't of his daughter? If they needed any additional information, they would call Gail for her input. Because Ms. Thomas left earlier for work, she claimed she never knew anything. Gail's mother said when Nee-Nee came over, she basically was content playing with Gail and pretending she belonged to a loving family with no expectations. She was using our house as a refuge from the evils of her father; this was her safe place.

Suddenly a dark sedan pulled in front of Gail's house. "I wonder who that is," said Gail as she stood in front of the glass door. A tall lady in a blue suit got out of the running car and headed towards the Thomas house with a small bag. Gail went out onto the porch to get a better look. She watched the lady until she walked into the Thomas house. She sat on her steps wondering what was going on inside. A tapping noise began to get louder and Gail started to investigate its origin. She headed towards the car and noticed Nee-Nee sitting in the back seat tapping a barrette against the window. "Nee-Nee, Let the window down," Gail motioned. "I can't," Nee-Nee slowly mouthed. "I'll miss you most of all Gail. Maybe one day we'll meet again." Gail said loudly, "I'll miss you too – be good." Nee-Nee started talking about how she wanted to be one of Gail's first students in her English class. Gail couldn't understand her muffled ramblings, so she motioned that she couldn't understand her. Just then the social worker was returning down the walk with a bag of Nee-Nee's things. "Hello, my name is Gail and I'm taking a social work class in college. Can't I even say goodbye to her?" The lady walked around Gail to get to the car. "Excuse me young lady, but we must go now." Gail moved back and began to think about the picture her brother took of them playing in her room. "Ma'am, can you wait just one minute while I run in the house and get something for Nee-Nee?" "One minute," the lady insisted. Gail came running out of the house with the framed picture; she wrote a note on the back:

> *"Nee-Nee, I will really miss you. Who will I play jacks and paper dolls with?*
> *I will never forget you – Love, Gail."*

From the driver's panel, the lady rolled Nee-Nee's window down; Gail looked at her for a few seconds and asked, "Are you alright?" Nee-Nee nodded lifelessly. Gail handed the picture to Nee-Nee and then leaned in the window and hugged her.

Chapter 17

"If it isn't love why does it hurt so bad, make me feel so sad inside..." New Edition

"What's your classification," the Registrar asked as Gail appeared to be in another world. "Miss," the Registrar repeated, "What's your classification?" Gail finally responded, "I'm a junior."

After locating her records and checking off a few boxes, the Registrar said, "Okay, your registration is complete, you may proceed to the Financial Aid and Work Study table. "Thank you." Gail said, as she moved slowly to the next table and got in line. There were 5 students in front of her: all of them looked like they had problems. One guy was rifling through stacks of receipts and forms. Another guy was visibly nervous, and the three girls just looked lost – must have been freshmen. Gail had a crush on a young man, Will Edwards, who she thought hung the moon and the stars. He was in a fraternity; he was vice president of the Student Government Association (SGA) and he played baseball. He was intelligent, articulate and very handsome. He wore shirt, tie and slacks almost every day. He had a hint of a mustache and his hair was always neatly coiffed; it looked neat and shiny like he just stepped off the cover of Black Enterprise magazine. She liked him so much but all he ever saw in her was as a friend. "What are you daydreaming about," Will tapped her on the shoulder and said. "You want to do something after we get our books and stuff?" Getting your textbooks and supplies was the last stop of the registration process. Gail loved hanging out with Will, even if his feelings were not the same as hers. "Sure," she beamed. Gail moved up in line. "Let's meet in the student center when we're done." "Okay," they both said. Will pushed her on her back and dashed off to the next table. Gail started thinking about what she would talk about and how she could make him look at her as a potential girlfriend instead of as just a friend. He did not have a girlfriend because he claimed he was too busy. Gail was in such a daze that she did not even notice two of her sorority sisters, Renee, and Crystal walking up to her. They had their textbooks, so they were done with registration. "Hi Sister Gail," said Renee, "Are you still drooling over Will"? Crystal, a senior cheerleader, popped her head in Gail's face and said, "there are guys who are just waiting for an opportunity to get with you." Gail burst out of her bubble and gave them a hug. "I do not know what y'all are talking about," Gail said. Out of the blue, she said, "Hey Zetas." They responded quickly, "Hmmm Yeah!" Crystal, who was very animated, jumped in with a suggestion, "Let's go get something to eat when you are done, and we can talk about your love life." "We can go to your favorite taco place," said Renee. "I also want some type of frozen, slushy drink," she added. Gail happily announced that she had plans. "Will wants to do something after registration, so he is going to meet me in the student center." "Okay, that's our signal," said Crystal. "Let's go because I'm starving like Marvin; let's get some soul food, added Renee with her tongue stuck out towards Gail. "I'll call y'all later," Gail said as she waved goodbye to them. "Hey Zetas," they chanted as they walked off.

Finally, Gail was at the front of the line. Ms. Carson, coach of the girl's basketball team was assisting the financial aid staff. Gail took her Health class and really enjoyed the class; she made an A. "Young lady," she said as she asked Gail for her registration paperwork by extending her hands. She leafed through the forms, initialed some areas, and printed off another form for Gail. "Take this supply allotment voucher to the bookstore; you have $500 to spend." "Thanks Ms. Carson," Gail said with elation. Gail gathered her forms and pulled out the voucher and the list of books she needed for her 5 classes. She could get her textbooks, a couple of sweatshirts and some school supplies. She would leave at least $100 in her bookstore account so she would be able to get miscellaneous items her professors may require later in the semester. "Your total comes to $289," said Ms. Brown, the bookstore manager. She had a sweet soft voice like Aunt Bee on the *Andy Griffith* show. "Your balance is $211 for the Fall; just show your student identification card for future purchases and we will be able to pull up your account on our new computerized system. Gail gathered the bags of books and supplies; she had 4 bags. "Thanks so much," Gail said, as she rushed upstairs to the student center. When she reached the student center lobby, she saw Will in some girl's face. Will ran over and hugged Gail excitedly. "Hey Gail, give me a raincheck for today and I'll make it up to you, okay." "Okay, no problem – what's up," Gail asked. "I called an emergency SGA meeting to discuss a few issues and we are going to meet now to avoid having to stay later." Will gave her a sad pitiful-looking face and clasped his hands together pleading for her forgiveness. "Okay, okay, I'll see you later," Gail said. She was disappointed, but she did not dare show it. Instead of sulking about it all, she bopped to the car and decided to go home and show all her books and stuff to her mother.

Chapter 18

"You got a fast car but is it fast enough so we can fly away…" Tracy Chapman

Will drove up in his silver convertible rabbit. Gail loved to see him driving up and down the streets because he looked so good in that car. She especially loved it when he came to visit her, and all the neighbors would be checking him out; they thought he was some rich college kid. Gail was sitting in the living room with her mother talking about her school schedule. Will jumped out of the car, he never used the door when the top was down. He was wearing some khaki cargo pants and a short yellow sleeve polo shirt. The tan deck shoes gave him the perfect preppy look. He came up to the door and rang the doorbell. Even though they were sitting right there, he could not see them sitting in the living room, through the storm door. Everybody liked Will and treated him like a member of the family. Alex opened the door, "Hey Will." "Hey Alex, is Gail here?" "She's around here somewhere, come in - just have a seat, I'll get her." Gail disappeared from the living room, but her mother was sitting quietly in a chair near the back. "Hi Ms. Quincy," Will said as he went over to give her a hug and kiss. "I know you're glad registration is over; it seems like it always takes so long," Ms. Quincy said. "Yes ma'am," Will said. "Did you get all the classes you wanted,' she asked. "Yes ma'am, I have a full load; I have 16 hours." Just then, Gail came from the bedroom walking hesitantly towards the living room. Gail gave Will a disgruntled look and he picked up on her disappointment. "Hey Gail," he pulled her close to him and proceeded to put her in a gentle headlock while giving her pretend *noogies*. Gail's mother headed towards the front door. "I'm going to sit on the porch, y'all are too silly." Will sat on the couch and pulled Gail down beside him. Both made a loud thud when they sat on the plastic covered couch. "Don't you think your mother should get rid of this plastic by now – all of y'all should know, by now, not to spill or eat anything in here." "Anyway," Gail said, "I thought you had an important SGA meeting." "I did and it's over." Will slowly opened his hands, "look what I got." He had 2 skinny cigars; they were dark brown with a shiny label and some clear plastic. "Let's go downtown by the river and smoke them. Ask your mother if you can go," Will insisted. "Okay!"

Gail rose and started yelling towards the front door, "Momma, Will and I are going downtown to smo," Will covered her mouth quickly. Her mother answered from the porch, "Y'all be careful downtown." They both laughed. Gail was rubbing the back of her legs; the plastic on the couch had left an impression from the seam. Gail was wearing a denim skirt and a sorority t-shirt. Will quickly stated, "You can't wear that shirt." "That is right, Gail said. "I can't be caught smoking in my sorority letters; I would hate to give the wrong impression of Zeta." A few minutes later, Gail came out wearing a red twinset; she took off the cardigan and draped it over her shoulders. "You look good in red," Will said. Gail felt tingly all over from that compliment and could not hide her satisfaction in knowing Will found her attractive. She beamed at him and took his hand. "Let's go!" They ran towards the car. Will and Gail were good friends and their friends and family knew that's all it was to them. The hugs and kisses were simply signs of platonic affection. They occasionally flirted with each other and they even kissed on the mouth many times, but it never amounted to anything. Girls at school would often ask Gail if they could talk to Will because they assumed, they were a couple. Gail would be upset over their assertive and aggressive behavior, but nonetheless explained that they were just friends. She hated that they disregarded her feelings but liked that they asked her for permission.

"Put your hands on the wheel." Will sped down Riverside drive with his arms stretched high above his head. "Weeee – do it, it's fun," he said. Gail began to hold her hands up and smiled at Will. "I can do it, but you need to drive carefully and safely with this precious cargo on board." He added, "Don't I know it." They both shouted, "Weeee!" Will found a nice secluded spot under the bridge; it was also close to the river. Gail did not want to smoke, but she wanted to do whatever Will wanted to do. He lit the 1st one and took a puff. The smell reminded Gail of her History professor, Dr. Newman. It was not a bad smell, but now Gail felt like Dr. Newman was somewhere in the vicinity peering at her over his glasses saying, "Young lady, is this really the right thing to do?" Dr. Newman was one of her favorite professors; he was deeply passionate about history.

"Try a puff," Will said as he handed her the cigar. Gail inhaled, exhaled, and inhaled again gearing up for the experience. "It's a cigar, not a marathon, "Will blurted out while watching her preparation exercise. "Just try it." Gail slowly put it up to her mouth and then pretended to be a classy movie star like Lauren Bacall or Marlene Dietrich. Then she did a Mae West impression "Come up and see me some time big boy," and took a puff. Before she could blow it out correctly, she started to cough and choke. She handed it back to Will and got out of the car. He watched Gail walk around blowing and spitting. He shook his head and took a few more puffs. "All that drama from one puff – give me a break, you are too dramatic." Gail was being overly dramatic but she loved the attention so she milked it as much as she could. When she finally looked up from her wrenching cough, Will was handing her a peppermint. "Thanks," Gail said.

They sat in the car and looked up quietly at the sky for what seemed like hours. Finally, Will broke the silence, by saying, "let's go watch the airplanes take off at the airport." "I'll even buy you some ice cream along the way," he said. "Sounds good to me," Gail said as she began to put her seatbelt on while straightening her clothes. Will slid down into his seat and tapped the cigar out. "We'll save this for next time." He found an envelope among his stuff in the back seat and placed both cigars in it. He put the envelope in his glove compartment and turned to Gail with a big grin. "Let's fly away together." All along the interstate, Gail had her eyes closed and enjoyed the wind on her face. Every now and then, she would look over at Will and he would give her an *I love being with you, too* smile. They stopped at a corner store and got some jumbo ice cream sandwiches with vanilla, chocolate, and strawberry ice cream in them. When they arrived near the airport landing; Will drove around for a good vantage spot. He got out of the car and ran around to open Gail's door. As soon as Gail got out of the car, Will hugged her tightly like he did not want to let her go. She liked it so she just held him close until he withdrew. Without uttering a word, he kissed her in the mouth; this time it was a long-wet kiss. He then led her to the back of the car and lifted her up on the trunk of the car. "This is the best seat in the house," Will said as he plopped Gail down gently. He climbed up next to her and began to lean back finishing the now melting ice cream sandwich. "Here one comes." The jet engine sound got closer and closer and then there it was over their heads flying high. "I wonder where they're going." Gail said. "I imagine it's going to California or Washington, DC." Will added, "How about Ohio or Arizona?" "Here comes another one, "Gail set up and said. "What if one just crashed and landed right in front of us," Will said. "That would be awful," Gail said sadly." "You're so sentimental," Will said, while poking Gail with his feet. "It's getting dark, we won't be able to see the planes in a minute." "Let's stay a little while longer," Gail insisted. "Okay, but don't start whining when bugs and other creatures of the night come out, Will said using a creepy voice. Gail slid off the car and got back in the car. Will got in with her. As the sun went down, Will laid his head on Gail's shoulder, and said, "I was just kidding – stop being so scary." Will turned towards Gail and lifted her head near his; he gave her a soft kiss on her forehead. He then kissed her nose and her chin. When he kissed Gail ever so lightly on her lips, she almost collapsed from the intensity. Will kissed her again long and passionately. Gail did not resist and before they knew it, they were making out like teenagers. Will ran his hand under Gail's skirt and pulled her underwear off. He was still kissing her the entire time. Gail felt a sensation that she never felt before. Will continued to stimulate Gail until she pushed his hand away. "I want you," Gail whispered in his ear. "Are you sure?" Will replied. "Yes," Gail said excitedly. Totally silent, they moved to the back seat at the same time. Will slowly unbuckled his belt, unsnapped his pants and quickly revealed his manhood. Most of the time, Will did not wear underwear because he said it was too restricting. When Will first told Gail, he did not wear underwear all the time, she asked him to prove it and he showed her his bare bottom. He wears underwear mostly in the Fall and Winter, but in the Summer – 8 out of 10 times, he is *au natural*. "Touch it," Will asked as he held her hand to guide it to its destination. Gail could not see a thing, but she felt a warm, firm sensation as he began to enter her. There was a bit of discomfort because this was her first time, but she was in such a euphoric state, she did not realize that during all the thrusts of passion, Will had asked her if she was a virgin. "Earth to Gail; are you alright?" "Yes, I'm okay; hold me tight," Gail said. She did not want Will to let her go, but he did and quickly. "We should go, I don't want your Momma fussing at me or you," Will said as he pulled himself out and began to put his clothes back on. Gail wondered what she did wrong, but she did not ask. She started to get herself together and then she realized she could not find her panties. Will put them on his face and sniffed them lovingly. "Are you looking for something?' "You're such a freak." Gail grabbed her wet panties and put them back on. She thought about her comment and realized it was too late to take it back, so she just grabbed Will's arm and said, "I'm just kidding." Will put on his seat belt as Gail got situated and appeared ready to go. "You know

I love you, don't you," Will said. "I love you too, Gail said sweetly. Will immediately added, "I don't want this to ruin our friendship. "I know what you mean, let's just take it one day at a time," insisted Gail. "No strings and no expectations. Will repeated it, "No strings and no expectations. Will drove off blaring J. Geil's band rocking hit, *Centerfold.*

Chapter 19

"I come home in the morning light, My mother says when you gonna live your life right…"Cyndi Lauper

"Are you ready? asked Gail as she held the phone. You have probably changed your outfit 5 times. I'll be over in a minute and we can decide together." Gail hung up the phone and shouted to her mother that she was going across the street to help Lori Ann decide what to wear to the EClub. The EClub – Enlisted Club was a club in Millington, 30 minutes from Memphis where many military guys, mostly Navy & Marines hung out in a relaxed, but controlled environment; the ratio was like 10:1 in their favor. Gail loved a man in uniform, plus she felt safe with the guys. Lori Ann liked hanging out there because she knew these enlisted guys had money and always wanted to spend it. According to her, "they didn't have anything else to do with it after they bought up all the jewelry and electronics." Gail's mother was happy that she spent some time with Lori Ann every now and then. She told Gail one day that Lori Ann would just be sitting on her porch sometimes staring into space. Lori Ann worked weekdays at a warehouse from 11a – 7p, so she could sleep late after partying. Lori Ann partied at least 3 nights a week. When she was not going to the EClub with Gail, she was hanging with ladies from her job. Gail generally went to school-sponsored parties once a month or so, but for the most part, she hung out with her sorority sisters in evenings, working on the newspaper staff, studying with classmates, tutoring Freshmen or doing work-study in the library. They always had a good time dancing, drinking, and talking with the sailors; they had the best stories.

"That is cute what you have on, wear that," Gail said. "I wear this to death," Lori Ann said as she turned all angles checking herself out in the floor length mirror. She was wearing a black satin vest over a pinstriped blouse with black & gray satin pants and some black patent leather stiletto heels. "I wear the dog and puppy out of this outfit. Let me change really quick." Lori Ann began stripping her clothes off. "Oh, Lori Ann, you and your country sayings, just hurry up and do that in the bathroom." "Gail, stop being so modest – we have the same thing; you just have more of it all. Smiling, Lori Ann swung her blouse at Gail's head. "Okay, this is it, I'm going to let that other outfit rest and breathe for a few weeks until I wear it again – although I do look good in it," Lori Ann said. Lori Ann started to pick up the satin outfit as though she were considering it again. "Let's go," Gail quickly said. She grabbed Lori Ann's hand, her purse, and the keys. "Do we need gas?" Gail asked. "I got $10 for you and $10 for me." "Sounds good," said Lori Ann. "I have $28, so that should get us to Millington, get us some drinks and get us some breakfast, if necessary," she said, smiling. If we are lucky, we will leave with $38. They would generally buy their 1st drink and after that, the guys would buy the rest of the drinks for the evening. "I don't need any gas, so let's go and jam that radio. Which cassette should I put in?" Gail asked as she rifled through Lori Ann's meager collection of Michael Jackson, Prince, Minnie Ripperton, Tina Turner, Hall & Oates, Bootsy, Commodores, Cyndi Lauper and others. "Just put in Cyndi Lauper for our traveling music and then we will groove with the Commodores," Gail said. Lori Ann said, "The ladies at work be tripping about my Cyndi Lauper cassette. I told them it was the jam. They told me I should get some J. Blackfoot and Barkays – you know some Memphis hits?" Gail nodded, yes, as the music started to play. Once they arrived, the club was packed with so many shades of men. It was a beautiful sight. Before they could find a table and sit down, guys were approaching them to dance or offering to buy them drinks. The attention was everything.

Chapter 20

"Heavenly father watching us all, we take from each other and give nothing at all…"
James Ingram and Michael McDonald

Crystal Vincent, one of Gail's sorority sisters was rushed to the hospital after complaining of headache and dizziness during graduation rehearsal. Crystal was an only child; she loved her sorority sisters very much because they were like sisters to her. Every time she was going somewhere, whether it was a trip to the Mall or to the post office, she would call at least 2 or 3 of them to hang with her for the company. Crystal told Gail everything; she confided in her about her complicated love life. Crystal did not have a boyfriend per se, the guy she liked, Wayne, was married with four children. He told her that his wife tricked him into marrying her by getting pregnant her senior year in high school. He knew he was not ready for marriage, but he wanted to do the right thing – they had three more children and he told Crystal that he has been stuck ever since. Crystal has "been with" Wayne Brewster for 2 ½ years. They met while she was trying to get some customer service assistance at an electronics store. He was working the floor when he noticed her impatient body language and offered his assistance. "What seems to be the problem?" Crystal walked up to the counter where he guided her and told him she was having problems setting her VCR. She showed him the brand she purchased and the receipt. He immediately knew her problem. "We have had lots of complaints on this model. I will be happy to make a service call, free of charge, to make the necessary adjustments in programming." Impatiently, he waited on her response with a grin. Crystal was a bit hesitant but agreed thinking she would invite some of her sorority sisters over for safety purposes. "Okay, that would be fine," Crystal said. He motioned for her to follow him and he gave her a clipboard to complete. "Fill out the top portion and I'll be right back," he said. Just as she was signing the form, Wayne took the form and while he was looking it over, he asked, "which do you prefer afternoon or evening?" Crystal said, "Evening is better for me, like 5 or 6 o'clock." Wayne looked at his schedule book and they agreed on Wednesday at 6. Crystal shook his hand and said, "Thanks so much; I will see you Wednesday."

"What does he look like?" Gail asked. Renee jumped in, "what's his body like – does he have a nice physique?" Crystal answered honesty, "I didn't pay attention to any of that; I was just trying to see about my VCR." Crystal started dusting around the tv/vcr area and tidying things up around her apartment. She did not want the guy to think she was a complete slob. "You must like him if you're cleaning up," said Gail. "I'm just tidying things up, so he'll be able to work without a lot of stuff in the way," said Crystal. "Well, what do you want us to do," Renee asked. "Just be here," Crystal said. "I do not know this guy and I do not feel safe having a stranger in my apartment all alone. He seems nice, but I don't want to take any chances. Crazy things are happening everywhere." Crystal was a huge Janet Jackson fan; she loved her since she was Penny on *Good Times*. Crystal was wearing black jeans, black cat t-shirt and a black hat. She was even wearing hoop earrings; one with a key dangling from it. This was her favorite casual outfit and she knew she looked good in it. *Ding ding Ding* The doorbell rang.

Crystal opened the door; it was Wayne. "Hello, come on in," she said. "We're just having some girl time playing Scattegories in the floor. The girls said in unison, "Hey." Wayne said, "Hello," in a reserved tone. Crystal pointed towards her bedroom, "the VCR is in this room – I really appreciate you coming." Wayne followed her and immediately took off his jacket, got on his knees and started to work. "I'll just leave you and you can call me when you need me." "You need to stay so you can see how to do this," he said in an authoritative tone. "Okay," Crystal said as she plopped down on the bed. He began to turn the small entertainment center around so he could get to the cords and to the back of the television. Wayne worked for 20 minutes while Crystal sat on the bed watching him. She noticed his features. He had freckled fair skin with curly brown hair in a fade and he had greenish brown eyes. He had a hint of a mustache and he was well shaven. He had a strong manly physique; he was a very handsome man. She remembered his hand being soft when she shook it and thought he will not be the one coming to do the service call. He wore tinted glasses and they gave him a hint of mystery. He looked exceptionally clean; his clothes were crisp and fitted nicely. He also smelled good, not overpowering, but he was wearing a nice cologne. Crystal suddenly was impressed with this man in her bedroom. He rose for a quick break and she said, "I missed my soap opera for the last 3 days and I am having withdrawal symptoms." She was sorry she picked that topic because she thought he would think she was shallow, but instead he said, "I bet you watch Young & The Restless." Crystal said, "No, I watch All My Children." "Oh, you like Erica Kane and the folks in Pine Valley, huh?" Crystal was amused at his knowledge of the soap and started to talk about her soap as though he were familiar with the various storylines. "Hold up, I don't know about all of that, just a little bit." They smiled at each other and realized they just had a moment. She heard the girls giggling in the other room. "Okay, now I'm ready to show you how to set your VCR to record your soap and other favorite shows. You might want to get a pad and pencil. Crystal grabbed her book bag in the corner and pulled out a legal pad and pen. "Are you in college," Wayne asked. "Yes, I'm a junior at LeMoyne-Owen College majoring in English," Crystal proudly admitted. "No wonder you can't figure this out – you got too much book sense." Wayne said with a smirky smile. "I really did try to figure it out – I read and re-read the manual." "I'm just messing with you," Wayne said. "I told you this model had some faulty issues that you would have never found if you hadn't asked for help." "Okay, this is what you need to do first – choose the day, time and channel." Crystal took copious notes and before she knew it, they were sitting in the floor together. Just then her sorority sisters came in to announce that they were leaving. "Do y'all have to leave now?" Crystal said. Wayne said quickly, "I promise not to chop her up in hundreds of pieces." Gail said, "You better not because we know where you work, and I jotted down your car license tag number." "Your girls got your back, don't they?" "Always," Crystal said as she quickly got up to walk them to the door. "I'll be right back," she told Wayne.

When she came back, Wayne was packing his gear. Crystal was a little disappointed that he was finished because she was just starting to enjoy his company. "I think you're all set - your shows should record as planned," Wayne said. "Even if your power goes out or anything, it will reset itself once the power comes back on, so you won't have to worry about resetting it, but it looked like you took good notes." Crystal began to put things back on the entertainment center as Wayne began to put on his jacket. "Well, it was so nice to meet you and I appreciate you coming out to help me with my VCR problems." Wayne opened his portfolio and pulled out a work order form. "If you would just sign this so my boss will know that I made a service call, I appreciate it." Crystal signed the form and they headed towards the door. She noticed Wayne looking in the living room. Gail and Renee left the Scattergories cards in the floor; they also left their cups and opened bags of chips and cookies in the floor. "You tell your sorority sisters to clean up after themselves next time they come over," he said. Crystal was opening the door, "Okay, I will." "Lock this door, now and be safe," he said sounding like somebody's Daddy. "Okay, you be careful, too, and thanks." Crystal said.

It had been 6 months since Crystal had been in this electronics store. She walked around the store with Gail and Renee. Renee was looking for a video camera so she could record her sister's baby shower. Each of her brothers and sisters gave her some money to purchase it. The ones that she saw cost $300 - $400. "Hello ladies," they heard a familiar voice say. They all turned around to see Wayne. "Hey," they said in unison just like the 1st night they met. "How's your VCR doing; is it recording everything like it's supposed to do," he turned to Crystal and asked. "Yes, it is doing simply fine, thank you for asking. "What's that cologne you're wearing, it smells really good – real manly." "If I told you I would have to kill you, Wayne said in a sneaky voice. Actually, I am not wearing any cologne, it is my aftershave. You look nice tonight, what are y'all up to tonight?" "Hello, we need some help," Renee interrupted. "I need a video camera – nothing too expensive and nothing too difficult to operate." "I think I know exactly what you need," Wayne said as he walked them towards the video cameras. "This model is our most popular; it is great for recording school programs, parties or small events and it's only $295. "Sounds good to me, because I only have $350 – I'll take it," Renee said. "You are easy," Wayne said. Crystal leaned in towards Wayne and added quietly, "If you only knew." They smiled at each other and everybody proceeded to the register so he could ring up Renee's purchase. Wayne punched in a few numbers and gave Renee the final cost. She handed him cash and smiled because she had some money left over. He put a "PAID" sticker on the video camera box and handed Renee the box and the receipt. "Well, it was great seeing you ladies again. Be sure and stop by and ask for me for your next electronics purchase." Wayne said. They all smiled and said, "kay, bye."

Gail went home to help her mother make cupcakes for her Sunday school class. Renee went home to show her brothers and sisters what a great bargain she got. Crystal headed home to catch her soaps – she was a couple of days behind. When Crystal got home, she had a message on her answering machine. *It sure was great seeing you this evening – you looked gorgeous. You look good in orange – it makes you look so radiant. I would love to see you again in a less official capacity. Call me, you know the number.* Crystal recognized Wayne's voice and could not help but smile at such a sweet message. She rewound it and listened one more time as she turned the television on. As she took off her shoes and clothes, she thought about Wayne's ability to get along with anybody, his pleasing personality, his kind-hearted nature, and his sexy lips. She slipped on a nightshirt and proceeded to start the VCR so she could watch her soaps. She went to put some popcorn in the microwave when she heard static coming from the bedroom. She went to see what was going on and all she saw was static on the screen. "Oh no, now what?" Crystal turned it off and on – plugged it and unplugged it – made sure wires were in the right place, but still no soap. She looked at the time and realized the electronics store was still open. She did not want to talk to Wayne, because she didn't want him to think she was calling for him. She remembered him saying earlier that he was leaving at 8; it was now 8:30. She found the number to customer service on her refrigerator and proceeded to call. "Customer Service, may I help you." Crystal didn't recognize the voice, so she told the representative her issue. She went on nonstop for about 10 minutes when the voice on the other end said, "I'll be right there." Crystal realized it was Wayne and before she could object to his forwardness, she said "okay."

Chapter 21

*"Stuck on you, I've got this feeling down deep in
my soul that I just can't lose…"* The Commodores

Crystal changed into her black jeans and an orange sorority t-shirt.
She did not put on any shoes; she wanted her orange marmalade
toenail polish to show. She began to tidy up the living room and
bedroom because those would be the two places Wayne would see.
She also cleaned the bathroom just in case he needed to use it. She
removed the curling iron from the sink and placed her basket of
toiletries under the cabinet. She thought to herself why am I doing
all of this – it is just a service call. She then heard another voice
whisper, or is it? The doorbell rang. She hesitantly answered it. As
she opened the door, she saw a bouquet of raisinettes, goobers and
popcorn wrapped in an orange, blue and white bow. Wayne peered
over the bouquet and said, "I'm here to fix your problem, but this
time, I want to watch the soap with you. I'm curious as to what is so
fascinating about them." Crystal showed him to the bedroom and
said, "You're awfully forward tonight. I thought you were getting off
at 8:30." Wayne looked shocked that she remembered his schedule.
"Well, I couldn't leave; I had to wait until 9:00. My Manager was
running late from visiting another store, but he came just in time
to close. If he had come on time, I would have missed your call."
Crystal looked at him as he started to work on the VCR. She again
noticed that wonderful manly smell of his aftershave. "Can you fix

it," she said. Wayne looked puzzled, "You must have done something to this VCR because it was programmed perfectly to record your soaps daily." He started to pull the entertainment center from the wall and check the connections. "Oh, here's your problem." He got some tools out of his bag, did some tweaking and before she knew it, Crystal, who was folding clothes while he worked, heard the theme music from *All My Children*. She jumped up and gave him a hug of thanks. "You're welcome," Wayne said. He did not let her go too readily; they looked at each other longingly. Crystal changed the awkward mood by saying, "Okay, I'll let you watch this episode with me, but you have to promise not to ask too many questions or talk too much." "I promise, Wayne said, but "what about the snacks?" "Okay and thanks, I'll get the snacks ready," she scooped them up off the bed, "while you put my entertainment center back in place," Crystal said. Crystal bopped to the kitchen with the bouquet of goodies. She was reaching for a bowl to put the chocolates in when she felt a hand reach around her waist. She turned around quickly, and Wayne kissed her softly. "Thanks for letting me stay a while," he said as he walked back towards the bedroom. Crystal thought should I be offended by such forwardness and say something or just revel in the moment because the kiss was nice. She decided to revel in the moment. She looked around at her kitchen with dishes in the sink and cups on the counter. "I knew I should have straightened up in here, too." When she got back to the bedroom, Wayne had put some pillows on the floor. "Come on down here," he said. She only had one chair in her bedroom, and it was a desk chair, so it was not too comfortable. Sitting on the bed certainly was not a good option, so she was glad Wayne took the initiative with the pillows. She plopped down and positioned the snacks between them. "Oh, I forgot to get something to drink," Crystal said as she started to get up. "Wait a minute, "Wayne said. He got up and grabbed his bag; he pulled out a bottle of sparkling peach wine. "I must say," Crystal said as she got up to go get some glasses, "you certainly have thought of everything. I am impressed with your confidence. I hope this wine is good." "I think you'll like it," Wayne said. Crystal came back with two wine glasses and some napkins. Wayne opened the wine and began to pour. He said, "You know you really fascinate me and your voice drives me crazy; I have never met anyone like you." "Is that good or bad," Crystal asked. "It's good because I want to know more about you – what are you afraid of – what is your favorite color – what is your favorite food – do you go to church – where do you work – do you have a boyfriend and ..." Crystal smiled because he had a kind of bad boy persona that was hard core and cute at the same time. "Let me see," Crystal began to answer the questions: I'm afraid of spiders and rodents, My favorite color is orange, My favorite food is chicken alfredo, I go to the same church I got baptized at when I was 10, I work at the public library part-time and I'm a full-time student at LeMoyne-Owen College, I *had* a boyfriend – long story, and what about you, same questions except change the boyfriend to girlfriend – obviously. Wayne looked at her, gently grabbed her face in the palm of his hands and said, "I really like you." He kissed her softly on the lips. "I'm from Memphis – south Memphis to be exact, I'm afraid of missed opportunities, My favorite color is black, My favorite food is barbeque, I go to church and I was baptized when I was 10 too, you know where I work, but I am studying to be an EMT Emergency Medical Technician, I don't have a girlfriend, but I do have a wife and 4 kids. Crystal looked at him harshly and said, "This isn't right; I appreciate your honesty, but I must ask you to leave now." Crystal started to get up, but Wayne pulled her back down closer to him. "Please let me explain the situation." Wayne said he and his wife got married straight out of high school because she got pregnant in their senior year. He wanted to do the right thing, so he married her and then she got pregnant again and again. He felt trapped, but he did not want to leave his children. His relationship with his wife is lacking so much passion that he can barely speak about the many times he has had to force himself just to have sex with her. He said she is a good mother, but she is not a good wife. Further, she never cleans the house the way he thinks it should be done. He does most of the cooking and the cleaning. Crystal listened, but she still did not think being hugged up on her bedroom floor with a married man was the right thing to do. She thanked Wayne for making a "house call," and started to show him to the door. "Don't turn me away," he said. "I want to be your man." "How can you be my man when you are married?" Crystal asked. "I'm really hurt that you lead me on like this." Wayne stopped her in the hallway, "let me prove to you that I can be your man; give me a chance." He pulled her close and began to kiss her long and hard. Crystal could not resist his passion and intensity; she gave in and was lost in his kisses. For the next 6 months, Crystal and Wayne were inseparable. He came over almost every night after work. They would eat dinner together and watch movies and of course, All My Children recordings. Crystal would have to make him go home most nights because he never wanted to leave. They loved going to tourist-type places around the city; the zoo, museums, craft fairs and believe it or not, libraries. They were careful not to venture into places where they might see their co-workers, relatives, or friends.

One night when Crystal was cooking, Wayne came from behind and started kissing her neck. "When are you going to let me make love to you?" Crystal had reservations but slowly gave in to his pleas. Wayne picked her up and sat her on the kitchen counter. They kissed passionately. Wayne unbuttoned his shirt to reveal his spectacular physique. He had freckles on his chest that looked like little chocolate chips and she wanted a taste. He pulled Crystal's t-shirt off over her head to reveal an orange lace bra. He whispered, "Is everything in your sorority colors and do you have matching bottoms?" He began to kiss her chest and was about to undo her bra when Crystal stopped his hand. "Not in the kitchen," she said. She led him by his belt buckle to the bedroom. You could tell this love making was long overdue; the pent-up emotions were obvious as they explored each other's bodies. Wayne kissed and caressed every part of Crystal's body and she reeled with each sensual move. After the 2nd time, Wayne asked for some water. "Can a brother get some water? I need to build up my strength for round three." "What about dinner; I was making your favorite lasagna; I just need to add the ricotta cheese layer" Crystal added. "Okay, bring me some water please, finish the lasagna and while it's cooking, we can take a shower." Crystal smiled and said, "*Sounds like a plan Stan* oops I mean *you made it plain Wayne* or *that sounds insane Wayne* or I got it *Ok Wayne, you the Mane*." Wayne threw a pillow at Crystal as she stood in the doorway with her orange t-shirt on rambling off these silly phrases. "You are too funny, too fine and too quirky, I love you," said Wayne. Crystal smiled and yelled while walking towards the kitchen. "I love you, too." Crystal ran back in the bedroom and gave Wayne a kiss – "you got Boo-status, now." Wayne said, "What do I get to call you, now?" Crystal said, "Just keep calling me Baby. I love it when you call me, baby." "Okay Boo?" Crystal said. Wayne said, "Okay, Baby" "I cannot wait to tell Gail that you finally said, you loved me. She told me you would be the first to say it." Wayne mumbled, "Must you tell Gail everything?" and Crystal said, "Yes."

Chapter 22

"...Yes, He can mend what is broke, whatever is broke..." Mississippi Mass Choir

"Is she going to be okay?" Gail asked the nurse as she exited Crystal's room. "Are you a relative," the nurse asked. "No, I'm her sorority sister, but her parents are on their way – they are flying in from Nashville. Can we see her?" "I'm sorry Miss; I have to talk to her parents, first." The nurse patted her on the shoulder and walked away. Gail peeked in the door, but she could not see anything. She walked down the hall to the waiting room where the other sorority sisters and friends had gathered. She asked everyone to join hands and form a circle. Gail began to pray, "Lord, please take care of Crystal. You said where 2 or more are gathered in Your name, you will be in the midst. We need You to heal her today Lord. Our beautiful sister needs a blessing right now. Find the problem and fix it Lord. We know You can fix what is broken and we have faith that You will do it. Give the doctors the ability to heal her through you Lord. Please Lord: heal our sister that she may be whole again. We love You Lord and we give you all the praise and honor. We know we need You and we cannot get along without You. Please heal our sister, right now, in the name of Jesus, Amen. Everybody in the room started hugging and comforting each other. Everybody loved Crystal; they felt she did not deserve this pain. They waited and waited. Some folks had to leave, while others were steadily coming into the waiting room. It stayed packed until Crystal's parents arrived.

Gail was wrapped up in a blanket in the corner when she saw Crystal's parents walk past the waiting room. From the door, she watched them as they headed down the hall towards the nurses' station. The nurse walked up to them, talked to them briefly and motioned for them to have a seat. A tall man in scrubs approached them slowly, he must have been the doctor, he sat down with them and proceeded to explain her condition. Crystal had an aneurysm; there were no preexisting conditions that could have warned or prevented it from happening. She would require much rehabilitation because her left side had a temporary paralysis. The doctor could not say when she would regain the use of her left side. He could only tell them that her speech would be slurred for a few weeks, until she was completely stabilized, and all her vitals were back to normal. Crystal's parents embraced each other because they were happy it was not any worse. They all stood up and started to go towards Crystal's room. "Hi Mr. & Mrs. Vincent, we are in the waiting room, just wondering, how Crystal is," Gail asked. Mrs. Vincent said, "she's going to be just fine – we are going to see her now." Gail asked, "Can I come?" Mrs. Vincent looked at the doctor and he shook his head, no. "I'll be right down there to give you a full report once I visit with my little sweetpea, okay." Gail smiled and walked off. She sensed something was not quite right and hoped Mrs. Vincent wasn't lying about Crystal's condition.

When Gail got back to the waiting room, she explained to everyone that Crystal's parents were in with her and she would let us know something when she came out. She plopped down in the seat next to Renee. "I'm exhausted," Gail said. "This whole ordeal is not only stressful but draining – I feel like I ran a marathon or worked in a warehouse." "I want to get something to eat, but I want to wait on her mother to give tell us what's wrong with Crystal." Renee gets up, "I'll get you some chips or candy out of the vending machine. I saw one when I came in." Gail said "no, no, I'll wait and get some real food, some healthy food once I find out." She pulled Renee back down to her seat. "I'm glad her parents are here; I wouldn't want to be alone in a strange hospital," Renee said. "She must have been really lonely being an only child." "Why do you think she liked hanging out with us so much," Gail added. "Remember, she would always call us whenever she had something to do or somewhere to go." "We were her family," Renee said. "We *are* her family," Gail said. Suddenly, Renee sat up and said, "Did you call Wayne and tell him?"

Mrs. Vincent walked into the waiting room and everybody stood up. She thanked everyone for being there. She told them about Crystal's condition and how it would take all prayers to see her through these tough weeks ahead. All the students lined up to hug Mrs. Vincent and give her words of encouragement. "God will bring her out." "She a strong-willed young lady – she'll beat this." "She will make it through this just fine." "I know God will bring her through." "We will keep praying for her." "We love her so much – she's our sister – she'll be alright." "We prayed for her earlier and the Lord got us this far – He'll take us all the way." "Please call if you need anything," Renee said as she handed her a piece of paper with her phone number on it. Gail waited until everyone was gone before she asked Mrs. Vincent, "Can I see her?" "Gail, the doctor thinks it would be wise for you to wait a few days before you visit. You see, Crystal does not quite look like herself right now and she has all these tubes." Mrs. Vincent began to cry. She searched her purse for a tissue and began to wipe her eyes. Gail took her hand and guided her to a seat. "I just want Crystal to know we are here and that she is not alone. She did not like to be alone; she always wanted someone with her whenever she went anywhere. At first, we thought she was just trying to get to know us better, but later we realized, she did not like to be alone." Mrs. Vincent looked up, still wiping her nose, "she had a twin sister, you know." Gail heard Crystal mention it when they first met, but never in much detail – just that her twin sister did not survive childbirth. "Her name was going to be Diamond – both of my sparkling girls. I had plans to always make sure their outfits had sequins or rhinestones on them. I know that sounds as you kids say, lame, but I had big plans for them. When Diamond did not make it, I think Crystal felt the loss just as much as I did or perhaps more. We could not have any more children after that, so her fate as an only child was there. We tried to have cousins over as much as possible and we enrolled her in all kinds of stuff so she would be surrounded by kids all the time, but she still longed for a sibling, a special bond. She had friends in school, but never a close best friend. I was so happy when she joined the sorority; I knew this would give her some special relationships that would last a lifetime. You girls have certainly showed your love for her tonight." Mrs. Vincent began to cry again. "Can I see her," Gail asked again.

Mr. Vincent walked in to hear Gail's question. He interjected, "Gail, the doctors don't think it is good for her to have visitors right now; come back in a few days. Mrs. Vincent and Gail stood up together. "Herb, she just wants to see her for a minute; I don't see what harm it could do." Mr. Vincent sat down because he knew he was not going to win this argument. Mrs. Vincent led Gail down the hall to Crystal's room. Gail opened the door slowly. Mrs. Vincent followed her in but stayed in the back so Gail could have a private moment with Crystal. When Gail saw all the tubes, tears welled up in her eyes. There were so many things going on around Crystal that she could barely get to her. Finally, her eyes landed upon Crystal's face. It was distorted and she looked like she was in pain. She did not see the radiant, vibrant young lady who would always seem to bounce when she walked across campus. Gail regained her composure and began to talk to Crystal. She told her about how the waiting room was packed with her sorority sisters and friends. She told her how they formed a circle and prayed for her healing. She began to rub her arm and say, "we are all here for you, and we will not leave you." Gail began to sing the Destiny's Child song, *I'm A Survivor*. Mrs. Vincent began to cry, so she tip-toed out of the room.

Gail got in her car and started to cry. She did not have any tissue, so she used some fast-food napkins she found in her glove compartment. She had been holding it in for so long; she was trying to be strong for everybody else. She had faith that God would bring her friend through this storm and she was not worried about her recovery. She knew Crystal would recover 100%. When she got home, her mother left a note on her bed: *I saved you a plate of chicken, cabbage, macaroni, and corn bread. Please eat it. Crystal will be okay; I prayed for her. You are a great friend and I know Crystal loves you very much. Love, Mom*

It was now close to midnight, but Gail ate her dinner because she was hungry. She did not taste any of it, but she ate it all. She was tired, but for some reason, she was not sleepy. She lay across her bed and thumbed through an old *Ebony* magazine. She was not reading the articles or looking at the pictures; she was just going through the motion of turning the pages. She closed the magazine, put in a Sade cassette tape which was in the middle of one of her favorite songs by the sultry-voiced singer, *Sweetest Taboo;* she looked up at the ceiling. She started to ponder how she would break the news to Wayne. Of course, she could not call him earlier; she didn't have his home number anyway. She would have to wait until tomorrow when the store opened to try and reach him.

Chapter 23

"So true, funny how it seems"
Spandau Ballet

Brrrring…the alarm went off at 7:00 a.m. Gail had an 8:00 class. She slowly got up, put on her slippers, and looked out the window. Was last night for real; was her friend really in the hospital not able to move? It was a gray, gloomy Friday morning. According to weather reports, it was supposed to rain later in the evening, but it looked like the sky was about to open. January had been an unusually rainy month and as it ended, it was going to maintain its pattern. "Gail are you up?" her Mom said softly, but firmly. "Yes, ma'am, I'm up," said Gail. "Thanks for saving me some food last night, it was all too good." "Okay, baby you're welcome. Have a nice day, pay attention and good luck on that African American History test." Gail had totally forgotten about the test she had in African American History at 10:00. She was so wrapped up in Crystal's situation last night that she did not think about school or studying. She scrambled around looking for her book, notes, and index cards. Her Mom needed the car today, so it would work out fine – she could study on the bus. Gail started mumbling her day's events in her head, "I can study on the bus and then after my 1st class – I will have 40 minutes to really get some good uninterrupted study time – I'll go straight to the library not stopping for anyone or anything." "Thanks, Mom," Gail said as she hurriedly threw on some jeans and a sorority sweatshirt.

"Arrrgh, the light is out." Gail flicked the switch up and down as if it would magically make the light come back on in the bathroom. Gail's mother, annoyed with the flicking sound sat up in bed and said, "There are some bulbs in the back room." Gail quickly got the bulb and changed it. She went by her mother's room and said, "changed it." Before her mother could say anything, Gail was finished in the bathroom; she was gathering her books and heading towards the door. "Gotta go, see you later." "Be careful, call me if you need me to pick you up, I love you." Gail was out the door before her Mom finished the last word. She had two more hours to sleep before she had to get up for work. She laid there praying that her daughter would make it to the bus stop safely and then onto to school. She checked the clock to make sure the alarm would go off and then she snuggled under the covers and fell asleep.

"From Slavery to Freedom" read the elderly lady seated next to Gail. "That's a powerful title, is it a good book?" "Yes ma'am, it's my book for a history class I'm taking at LeMoyne-Owen College," Gail said proudly. "You in college, you look like you should still be in middle school," the lady said as she patted Gail's leg. "You keep on studying and do something with your life. You do not want to be like me riding the bus to some white folk's house – I been cooking and cleaning for them for close to 15 years now. You know what they gave me for Christmas?" Gail was looking through her note cards, but did not want to be rude, so she answered, "Ma'am." "A pretty Christmas sweater with shiny ornaments all over it, a $20 bus card and a 10-pound spiral-sliced honey ham. Ever had one of them hams? It fed all 6 of us plus we had some folks over the next day for breakfast – it fed us all. The Hensons ain't bad people; they just like things a certain way. They said nobody can cook and clean the way I can," the lady said proudly. Before Gail could open her mouth to let the lady know that she had a major test she needed to study for, the lady rose to push the signal to stop button. "It was nice talking to you," Gail said politely. "You too child, and good luck on that test you are studying for so hard." Gail watched the lady climb down the stairs slowly with a cane and 2 bags. She did not see any houses, so she knew the lady would have to walk a while just to get to the subdivision where she worked. Gail started to wonder about the lady and her family life. She seemed content with her job.

"Miss Gail," the bus driver said. Gail was in a complete daze gazing out the window thinking about the old lady. "Miss Gail, this is your school, isn't it?" Gail snapped out of it and was mad that she did not get any major studying done on the bus. "Thanks Mr. Mann." She bounced down the stairs off the bus and up the steps to the college. The college was situated in the middle of a prominent neighborhood with 7 buildings – two 3-columned white and brick buildings sat prominently in the middle of campus – one was the Humanities building, where Gail took most of her English classes and the other one was the Administration building. These two buildings looked like old antebellum mansions. To the left of those buildings were the Sciences Building, the Gym and the Student Center and to the right was the Arts building, the Library, the Counseling Center and the Health Center. Right next door was the church where they had Chapel services every Wednesday at 11:30a. The campus was busy; there was always something going on outside – a forum, a demonstration, an awareness program or a social, You could smell the coffee brewing from the kiosk outside and the students were lined up for the free brew. They always had fun extras during exam time. Breakfast bars compliments of the student government association, pizza night in the student center, extended hours in the library, stress-free zones in counseling center, free pencils from the bookstore and study sessions with seniors. The sororities and fraternities were also hosting Study Tips sessions. Gail loved the campus and the student-teacher ratio. As she walked towards the Honors building, she realized she would have to rely on those 40 non-stop minutes for studying. She would try and call Wayne after class.

Chapter 24

"...I don't care how you get here, just get here if you can..." Oleta Adams

Gail was sitting at Crystal's bedside, reviewing her history notes when she heard a tapping on the glass. It was Wayne; she called him earlier and he told her he would be there as soon as he could. Gail tip-toed outside to speak to Wayne. They hugged and Gail updated him on Crystal's condition. "Can I see her," he asked. "Yes, this is the perfect time because her parents left a little while ago for coffee break. They will be back in a few minutes, though." Wayne looked at Gail and grabbed her arm tightly. "Do they *know* about me?" Wayne put an emphasis on *know* because he wanted to know if Gail told them that he was married. "No, they don't *know* that you're married," Gail said nonchalantly. "They *know* you've been dating for almost a year and they *know* that Crystal loves you very much. They are anxious to meet you, but you might want to remove the wedding band beforehand." Wayne twisted the band around his finger vigorously, "I cannot think about that right now, I need to see my baby." Gail opened the door and waved him in like she was an usher showing a visitor to his seat. As Wayne walked in and saw all the equipment hooked up and tubes attached to Crystal, tears started to roll down his face. He glanced up and down at the young woman he had known as a radiant and vibrant soul. The woman he was looking at was pale, lifeless, and stoic. He bent over and whispered in her ear, "Hey baby." He kissed her on her forehead, her cheek, her nose, and her chin. He then gently rubbed her face with the back of his hand. He knew how much she liked that because she often told him how much she missed it when he was not there. "Baby, you got to come out of this. I need you so much." He grabbed her hand and put the other hand on top of it. "God, please don't take my baby away from me – heal her, in the name of Jesus." Wayne started to talk to Crystal about how they met and how she rejected him. "I am your man and I am not going anywhere." He grabbed her hand again, put his head to their hands and began to pray. While he was praying, he did not notice the parents walking in the room. They waited until they believed he finished and said, "You must be Wayne." Wayne stood up, wiped his eyes, and extended his hand to the couple. "Yes ma'am, I am Wayne, it's very nice to finally meet you." Mr. Vincent said, "We don't believe in handshakes, you are practically family." He pulled him in for a robust hug. Mrs. Vincent hugged him next with the same vigor. "Our girl will be simply fine; she is going through a rough patch and will need some major support. Will you be there for her, son?" Mr. Vincent asked. "Yes sir," Wayne said. "I am not going anywhere."

Suddenly, the machines started beeping and Crystal's eyes opened and closed uncontrollably. Crystal's Mom ran outside and yelled for help. "We need a nurse; we need a doctor in here - we need some help in here!" The doctor came in followed by two nurses. He checked the machines and then looked at Crystal. The nurses shooed everyone out of the room while he assessed Crystal's condition. Mr. Vincent and Wayne paced the floor while Mrs. Vincent and Gail sat quietly together in the waiting room. Wayne checked his watch a couple of times. The 3rd time, Mr. Vincent asked, "Is there somewhere else you need to be?" "No sir," Wayne answered, "I am just wondering why it is taking so long." But Wayne was supposed to be somewhere in an hour; he was supposed to go to his son's soccer tryouts. They had been practicing every day after school so he could make the community team. Even though his son was only 8, he was anxious to make the team and start playing because he loved the game. His wife allowed him to play soccer because it was not as much of a contact sport like football. She said she did not want him to get hurt playing football. Wayne tried to explain that soccer is a contact sport and that it can be just as grueling. Wayne felt anxiety as he waited to hear the doctor's diagnosis – he could not leave Crystal, but he could not let his son, down, either. As he paced the floor, he folded his arms carefully so not to reveal his wedding band. Finally, the doctor came out with a promising look on his face. "We've had a breakthrough; she came out of the comatose state and is now slowing taking in her surroundings. "Can we see her?" Wayne asked. "Parents first," the doctor insisted. The doctor added, "You may see some minor paralysis on the left side, but hopefully this condition will go away with rehabilitation." As the parents walked down the hall to Crystal's room, they turned around and beckoned for Wayne to come join them. He ran towards them like a boy about to ride a rollercoaster. Gail sat there and said, "thank you God." She went to find a pay phone so she could call her mother and everybody to tell them that Crystal was going to be okay.

Chapter 25

..." Electric word life – It means forever and that's a mighty long time...." Prince

Lori Ann was walking to her car from the warehouse. It had been a long work week; she was happy it was Friday. Two of her co-workers walking behind her said, "Lori Ann, are you and Gail going to the E Club tonight?" "No, I haven't seen Gail in a while; she's doing her college thing." One of the ladies said, "I guess she forgot all about you, huh?" Lori Ann quickly responded, "best friends never forget each other." She got in her car, put in a Cyndi Lauper cassette tape and *True Colors* started to play, "*You with the sad eyes, don't be unhappy can't remember when I last saw you laughing...*" Lori Ann drove quickly out of the parking lot. When she got home, her little brother was in the living room with the street's known drug dealer. "What is he doing here? You know you have sickle cell and shouldn't be doing any drugs." "We're just talking," Dennis said. Dennis Johnson was the dealer for the whole street. He had kids making deliveries to schools and women doing pickups from corners. He always had the "good stuff." He did not look like the stereotypical drug dealer, in fact, if you did not know him, you would think he was a college student. He was always clean shaven, smartly dressed and his nails were perfectly manicured. He was not bad looking, just bad.

Dennis repeated, "We are just talking." Lori Ann huffed by and said, "that's generally how it starts." She started to walk towards her bedroom and Dennis added, "where are you going pretty lady – let me talk to you." Lori Ann was tired and did not have time for any nonsense, so she ignored him and kept walking towards her room. When she got to her room, in the back of the house, she turned on the television and her stereo. She pulled off her dusty clothes and put on a long t-shirt and some shorts while she got her things ready for her shower. Just as she was taking her clothes to the washing machine, Dennis popped up. "What are you doing tonight pretty lady; I would love to take you to dinner and a movie." Lori Ann turned around and said, "I am not going anywhere with you. I might get shot while they are aiming at you. A lot of people want to kill you and I don't want to get caught in the crossfire." Dennis laughed annoyingly, "That was a low blow." Lori Ann added, "the truth hurts." "We could go to College Circle; nobody knows me there; it's just a bunch of book heads that hang out there." Lori Ann had heard Gail mention College Circle lots of times and she always wanted to go and be a part of the "scene." Gail invited her to come along a couple of times when her sorority sisters were with her, but she did not like them. She thought they were too superficial. "Okay, let me shower and put on some preppy clothes," Lori Ann said. She ran through the beads with sudden excitement. After a quick shower, she put on a nice V-necked sweater, a skirt, some leotards, and some heels. She walked towards the living room slowly as though she were making some type of entrance. No one was in the living room. She called to her brother, "where's Dennis?" Her brother came out of his room, looking dazed and said, "He said he will be back to pick you u p in 30 minutes. He said something about putting on preppy clothes." Lori Ann smiled and headed back to her room to get some more mirror time. As she was looking at herself in the mirror, she began to wonder if she was excited about going on a date with Dennis or about finally getting to see College Circle. She looked in the mirror and said aloud, "College Circle." "Knock, knock, knock," Dennis said as he poked his head between the curtain of beads. "Are you ready, pretty lady?" Lori Ann turned around slowly, "do I look like I'm ready." Before Dennis could answer, she pushed him out and said, "Let's go, I'm starving like Marvin." Lori Ann kissed her mother as she passed her in the kitchen. "I'll be home later; Dennis is taking me out. Her mother was cleaning greens over the sink but looked up when she heard Dennis' name. She could tell her mother wanted to say something, but she held her tongue and continued cleaning the greens. "Don't stay out all night and please be careful," she said.

Chapter 26

"We caught eyes for a moment and that was that..." L L Cool J

"You look nice, did you change just for me or did you get roughed up," Lori Ann said. Dennis smiled and said, "When are you going to cut me some slack? I wanted to look good for you." "Okay, I'm going to pretend, just for tonight, that I don't know you're the main drug dealer on Dunbar street. I am going to pretend that I have not heard rumors about you giving drugs to kids. I am going to pretend that I didn't hear about you beating up some teenagers because they couldn't pay for their habit. I just want you to know that I don't plan on getting caught up in any of that mess." Dennis was visibly irritated, but said, "You be Cathy College and I'll be Joe College. What do you want to do first?" Lori Ann excitedly said, "I want some of the famous deep-dish pizza; I've heard people talking about it as being soooo good." Dennis put his left signal on. "We're here. College Circle: where geeks, jocks and Greeks hang out." Lori Ann sat up and was in awe of the sights. It was a circular plaza with shops, boutiques, and stores all around. In the center was a movie theater; it had only 5 screens, but it looked huge. Lori Ann read the marquee to see what was playing; they were showing horror classics Amityville Horror, The Omen, Carrie, Rosemary's Baby and The Exorcist. "Do you like horror movies," she asked Dennis. He looked at her and said, "I live a horror movie every day." Lori Ann was still

111

looking around in awe; she was not paying attention to Dennis or to his snide comment. This College Circle was everything Gail said it was and more. "There it is, let's go to Barb's Beauty Shop. They pulled into a parking space and Lori Ann could hardly wait to go inside. She sat there until Dennis came around and opened her door. He helped her out of the car. "Pretty lady, you're already pretty, besides, I thought you were hungry," Dennis said." Lori Ann grabbed his arm and pulled him towards the shop. "It is a restaurant, but it used to be a beauty shop a long time ago. They just kept the sign because it was so cool and I heard that on the inside they still have booths and big mirrors. I also heard that they make the best deep-dish pizza. Let's go, let's go." Dennis straightened his clothes back in shape that Lori Ann had tugged on and said, "okay, okay, calm down, let's go to the beauty shop." He glanced back at his car. He was proud of his gray Mustang; he had it washed at least once a week. The inside was spotless, and it had a nice cherry smell. When Lori Ann saw him "doing business," he was always in a black Ford pickup truck. All she ever noticed was the shiny 3D box hanging from his rearview mirror. If the sun hit it exactly right, it would look like it was shooting colored beams. As they walked inside the restaurant, they saw a sign that said, *Seat Yourselves – We'll Be Right With You.* Lori Ann headed for a quiet booth in the corner where she could check out all the action of the restaurant. Dennis let her get seated first and she sat down with a plop. "This place is so great." Dennis looked around as though he was checking to see if he knew anyone. He did not recognize anybody. Dennis responded, "Yeah, these thick glass booths are definitely from back in the day. Look at those razor straps on the wall." Just then a male waiter with sandy red hair and bushy sandy red eyebrows approached their table. He looked all of 18 years old with red freckles or maybe he was 21, since he had a hint of a mustache.

"Hi, my name is Buzz, I'll be your waiter. Our specials today are up on the chalkboard over there," he pointed. "They are deep dish lasagna, pasta primo vera and smothered ravioli. Of course, you can always order our famous deep-dish pizza with your choice of toppings." He points to the pizza sizes on the menu and then hears someone calling him. He holds up a finger and tells them he will be right back. "Everything looks so good, what do you want," Lori Ann asked. Dennis smiled as he answered this open-ended question - "What I want is not on the menu. Get what you want, and I'll have the same." Lori Ann smiled and studied the menu closely. When the waiter came back for their order, she blurted out, "We'll have a medium deep-dish pizza with pepperoni, Italian sausage and mushrooms, the salad bar and 2 sodas." She glanced over at Dennis for his approval. He nodded and continued looking at her like a lovesick puppy dog. Buzz took the menus and said, "Help yourselves to the salad bar, I'll put this pizza order in and bring your cups right over. The soda fountain is behind the salad bar." When the waiter walked off, Lori Ann said, "This place is so cool." Dennis started to get up from the table. He was a little uncomfortable, but he did not want Lori Ann to know. "Let's go get our salads," he said. Lori Ann walked towards the salad bar; she wondered if she had made a mistake coming with Dennis. He had been nothing, but a gentleman and he did not use any profanity around her. She was enjoying his company, so why did she suddenly feel uneasy about him? She shook it off as *first date nervousness* and started to fill her salad bowl. The little brown bowl seemed small, but surprisingly held a lot. "I guess you like mushrooms," Dennis said as he piled some on top of his bed of lettuce. "Me, too – I can make a mean mushroom cheeseburger." Dennis nudged her as he moved down the salad bar line. Lori Ann nudged him back and said, "You better watch out man." They finished making their salads and headed to their table. Dennis asked, "What kind of drink do you want?" "I'll get it while I get mine." He reached for her cup. "No, thank you, I want to make a special mixture. Use ginger ale for half with a little fruit punch and a hint of cola." "I'm sure I can do that," Dennis said. "Okay, go for it," Lori Ann said as she pushed her cup towards him. As Dennis walked off, she began to wonder how such a nice guy ended up as a drug dealer. He obviously had some good manners and knew how to treat a lady. She was having a good time. When Dennis returned with the drinks, he placed Lori Ann's drink carefully in front of her and handed her a straw. Lori Ann gently removed the straw paper, placed her straw in the drink and sipped cautiously. "Not bad," she said. "I'm glad you like it." Just then the waiter popped by to say the pizza was almost ready. Lori Ann and Dennis ate their salads quietly. They looked at each other periodically and smiled, but for the most part, they did not say much. Dennis had bleu cheese dressing on his salad and when Lori Ann noticed some of it was in the corner of his mouth, she called his attention to it. "You've got some dressing in the corner of your mouth." Dennis taking another opportunity to use his quick wit said, "Why don't you come over here and kiss it off for me." Lori Ann did not know what to say, luckily, she didn't have to respond. The waiter brought the pizza to the table; it was piping hot. He also put a small dish of fried mushrooms next to it. "We didn't order this," Lori Ann quickly said. "I ordered them," said Dennis. "Do you like horseradish sauce?" "Yes, I do, thanks," Lori Ann anxiously said. She thought about ordering them earlier but did not want to seem greedy.

"Let's eat up, the movie starts in an hour," Dennis said. They ate and talked for what seemed like hours. The fried mushrooms were obviously the conversation icebreaker because once they talked about how good they were, they went on from there. They had so much in common. They talked about folks in the neighborhood, the school teams, the current topics in the news and relationships. "So, who is that girl who always rides with you while you're conducting business?" Lori Ann asked as she sipped on her soda. "That is my cousin, Bae-Bae, she just graduated from high school; she likes to ride with me. She's going to college in the Fall." Lori Ann sat back in the booth and asked, "Does she know what you're going when you're riding around." Dennis answered quickly, "she knows." He looks around the restaurant and attempts to change the subject. "I wonder what that couple is arguing about." Lori Ann looked at him, knowing his plan and said, "Okay, I'll play… hmmm, he looks pretty mad and so does she. I guess they are mad because one has some secrets that the other just found out. Maybe it is a lover's quarrel, probably over some stupid issue like he was looking at her look at another guy the wrong way." "Sounds like you've been in that boat before," Dennis said as he leered over his glasses. "Well, I've been accused of being a flirt before and I can't help it if I'm friendly." "There's a difference in being friendly and *friendly*, Dennis said as he arched his back, brushed back his imaginary hair and blinked his eyes. Lori Ann twisted and turned trying to not be visibly amused and mad at the same time. She hesitantly said, "You're crazy." "Crazy about you," Dennis whispered. They ate the last of the pizza, all of the mushrooms and slurped down their sodas. Dennis looked at the bill, put down the exact amount first and added a $5 tip. "Alright, let's go see this scary flick," Dennis said as he began to get up from the table. Lori Ann jumped up and said, "Yeah, let's go." She reached for his hand and as soon as he adjusted his shirt, he grabbed her hand to exit.

Chapter 27

"When we met I always knew I would feel the magic for you…" Anita Baker

Dennis and Lori Ann dated for months before they admitted to each other and others that they were a couple. He met her for lunch during the week, he called her on her job throughout the day and he was often waiting in the parking lot when she got off. Everybody knew him by name at her job and Lori Ann was proud of the fact that people knew she had a boyfriend. He was friendly to everybody and he knew many of their names. Her family liked him and even let him spend the night in Lori Ann's room from time to time. He walked around the house like he lived there – raiding the fridge, making burgers, or just sitting around talking. He did not bring his *work* in the house and for the most part, he was a nice guy. They spent most of their weekends together doing unusual things like riding the trolley downtown or driving across the bridge to Arkansas. One weekend, they checked into a hotel and pretended to be from out-of-town. They even changed their accents to a more southern one. They told anybody who asked that they were cousins Jim and Kim from Alabama and that they were in town for their dear Aunt's funeral. They said Aunt Jessica, who they only visited once or twice, had loads of money, so they came to hear if she left them anything. She did not have a will, but her only child, Jesse Joe was going to divide up some of her belongings amongst family. They had loads

116

of fun with the hoax because both had vivid imaginations. Dennis'
work never interfered with their time together.

When Dennis' pager went off, Lori Ann would give him a look
and he would simply look at her and say, "I'll be right back." He
would never handle his "business" in front of her, which Lori Ann
thought was respectful in some sense. Most times Dennis would
come back and say, "Ok, where were we?" and things would be back
to normal. This time he had a worried look on his face and Lori Ann
could tell something was wrong. "Is it something you want to tell me
or is it anything I need to worry about right now?" "Don't worry, be
happy," Dennis said as he tried to change the subject by humming
a few bars of the song. Come on Cousin Kim, let's check out the
scenery across the street. Lori Ann perked up and said hunching her
shoulders, "Okay, Cousin Jim!" They walked across the street to an
old thrift store called, *Forget-Me-Nots & What-Nots*. It had anything
and everything you could think of from 1900 to present. They
walked around admiring the relics, sneaking kisses, and enjoying
each other's company.

> "*Times of good and bad, happy and sad…let's stay
> together*" Al Green

One rainy day when Lori Ann got off work, Dennis was not
there. She did not think anything of it initially until she noticed
when she got to her neighborhood, it was unusually barren. The rain
stopped and as she walked towards her house, she began to wonder
where Dennis could be on such a gloomy day. No one was on the
corners, porches, steps, etc. She went inside and asked had anyone
seen Dennis. Everyone was quiet. Lori Ann was starting to get upset
now, "I asked has anybody seen Dennis." "Did he call," she asked
looking towards her mother. "Nobody has rung that phone all day,
which is a good thing. No news is good news." She continued to
mumble something about why they call news bad while she walked
towards the kitchen. Her brother held his head down and shook it as

though he just could not tell her because he knew it would break her heart. "Do you know where he is Junior?" He sat down and started to tell her how the police came through the neighborhood around noon and took everybody that was on the corner and searched them. All of them had something on them, drugs, or weapons. If they didn't have anything on them, when they looked them up, they had outstanding warrants. Junior went on to say when he saw the police van coming down the street, he knew they were not leaving empty-handed. The police started asking questions around the neighborhood and somebody pointed Dennis out hanging on the corner. The next thing he knew, they were putting him in the police van with everybody else. They hooked up his truck and his car and towed it downtown with them. Lori Ann listened with amazement and disbelief. "I don't believe you," she yelled as she ran out of the house. She got in her car and drove around looking for Dennis. Some folks shouted: "they got your boyfriend, "now maybe we can get some peace and rest around here," "I'm glad they're gone" and "he's not here, he's gone to jail – where he belongs." "Where he belongs," Lori Ann repeated while walking in a daze back to the house. Junior met her at the door, "I told you."

Chapter 28

"Won't you hold me in your arms and keep me safe from harm?" Whitney Houston

"Will you accept the charges for inmate #2374 Johnson?" the voice on the other end of the phone said sternly. Lori Ann hung up quickly as though she had heard from a ghost. She sat on the couch and began to wonder what happened that Dennis had not contacted her in three weeks. She was clearly not in her right mind if she did not put two and two together. The phone rang again. She let it ring three times. Her mother shouted from the kitchen, "Lori Ann, the phone's ringing, please answer it; I'm elbow high in this bucket of chitterlings."

Lori Ann answered, "Hello." The operator said, "Will you accept the charges for inmate #2374 Dennis Johnson?" Lori said "Yes," and before she could brace herself, she heard Dennis' voice. "I miss you baby." "What happened," Lori asked calmly. "I don't have much time, so let's just say they're holding me on a technicality. Do you miss me baby?" Lori Ann did not know what to say, "of course I miss your peanut head, you were supposed to take me to that pottery making restaurant tonight." Dennis sighed, "Aww, that's right; I should be out in a few weeks, so don't go with anyone else, okay?" Lori Ann paused for a moment and at that moment, she realized she loved Dennis. He made her happy and he made her feel special. She depended on him for so much and it finally dawned on her how much she really *loved* him. "Dennis," she said slowly, "I'll wait for you.

A few weeks turned into a few months. Lori Ann found herself drawn to the correctional facility at least once a week to visit Dennis. Even though it was a two-hour drive, she passed the time by listening to the tapes he made for her: Jodeci, Mint Condition, New Edition and Earl Klugh. The visits were always fun and light in the beginning, but sad and gloomy when it was time for Lori Ann to leave. On her way home, Lori Ann stopped at a convenience store and picked up a six-pack of Cherry Coolers. She drank them down quickly as she drove down the highway blasting her music. Tears rolled down her face as memories of the good times with Dennis began to surface. She thought about how she despised him and his "profession." She questioned how she ended up with him and then she thought about how kind and gentle he was with her. She thought about their deep pillow talk conversations. He was totally the opposite of his bad-boy persona, with her. "37 miles to go," Lori Ann read the highway sign aloud sluggishly. She had one bottle left and she put it between her legs and held it there for a while. Once she realized it was cold, she put it in the cup holder. "Dennis, why did you leave me," she yelled. She wiped the tears from her eyes, grabbed some napkins to blow her nose and regained her composure. She put in a Cyndi Lauper tape and began to sing like she did when she was with Gail on those trips to the E club. "I'll call Gail when I get home and see if she wants to go out and do something. She's my best friend." Lori Ann started to cry again. She grabbed the bottle, popped the top and drank it down. She looked in the rearview mirror and noticed her own sad eyes. She needed someone or something to make her feel better. Dennis was gone and Gail was always too busy with her college friends. She did not hang out with the ladies at work much because they all seemed jealous of her. They talked about her skinny body, her skillet black skin, her bad boyfriend, etc. She liked going to the clubs with them because she did not have to talk to them – the music was always too loud to have an ongoing conversation.

When she turned on her street, someone was waving her down. It was one of Dennis' *associates*. Lori Ann slowed down and rolled her window down. "Hey Travis, what's up?" "Open the door, let's ride," he said. Lori Ann was in a funky mood, but said, "Okay, get in." Travis hopped in the front seat and bounced up and down like a child. He was only about 23 years old and he acted like he was 12. "What do you want, Travis, I just want to go home, take a shower, and go to bed, Lori Ann said as she drove slowly around the neighborhood. Travis was still bouncing around like a Mexican jumping bean. "Did you see Dennis? When is he getting out?" Lori Ann was annoyed but answered, "Yes, I saw Dennis and he still says it's going to be a few months." "Hasn't it been 4 months already," Travis added. "I know you miss him, y'all were hanging really tight the last few months before…" "What do you want Travis," Lori Ann shouted. "Calm down girl, I just wanted to know if Dennis gave you any instructions about what he wanted me to do with his stash. I know he didn't forget about it. Maybe, I will just go visit and find out myself. I could sell it, or I could keep it." Lori Ann looked surprised to hear that Dennis left something with Travis and not with her. But then again, he never mixed his business with their relationship – she appreciated him for that consideration. "I'm going back Friday, so you can come with me then," Lori Ann added. "No, I better go on my own; I don't want any trouble," Travis said, nervously. "Is that all you wanted, Travis – I have a date with my bed." "Just Calm Down – damn, calm down girl. I got something that would really relax you, Travis said as he reached in his side pants pocket. He pulled out a Ziploc bag of white pills. "Just take one when you get out of the shower and you will sleep like a baby." Lori Ann looked at him like he was crazy and said, "get out of my car with that stuff." Travis stuffed the Ziploc bag into Lori Ann's purse and got out. "Try them, you'll like them." When Lori Ann got home, she grabbed her purse and immediately put the Ziploc bag of bills in the zippered part of her purse. She walked straight back to her room without speaking. Her mother, who was at the sink washing dishes, said, "hello to you, too."

Chapter 29

"If I could save time in a bottle, the first thing that I'd like to do is to save every day 'til eternity passes away" Jim Croce

"Hello," Lori Ann answered her phone after it fell to the floor. The voice on the other end said, "Lori Ann, are you coming to work? You know you already missed three days this week and if you miss today, you're going to get written up." "I'm coming in," Lori Ann said as she hung up the phone, quickly. When she got up, she noticed a leg hanging out from under the covers. She did not remember anything about last night. She looked around for evidence of who this could be. She did see a t-shirt, jeans, and a bra in the floor – that was not her bra. Almost in complete amazement, Lori Ann sat down trying to put the pieces together. Suddenly, the covers began to unwrap this person's small frame. "Bae-Bae, what are you doing here?" Lori Ann asked. "Don't you remember, you said you would do anything for a little escape." Lori Ann said, "I thought you were going to college." Bae-Bae answered, "I went for a minute, but I needed some immediate gratification and Travis needed my help." Bae-Bae was no longer cute and feminine but totally hardcore. Because she helped Travis with Dennis' *business* while he was locked up, she felt she had to harden her look to get more respect on the street. Her original permed tresses were now cut in a natural coiffed style. The tear-drop earrings had changed to studs all around her ear and her perfectly arched eyebrows now had hoops above them. She stood in Lori Ann's bedroom in her panties and a tank top. As Bae-Bae was gathering her clothes off the floor, she said, "If you want some more this morning to help pick you up real fast, I know those fellas would love to come back and get with you because you definitely have skills." Lori Ann was disgusted; she held her stomach as though she was going to be sick. "Get out of here, I've got to get ready for work – I'm already late." Bae-Bae grabbed the rest of her things and headed towards the bathroom. "I'll be out in a few." Lori Ann rushed through her drawers to find some clothes to put on. She dressed hurriedly and told Bae-Bae to hurry up so she could lock up. Bae-Bae came out waving a bag of pills and crack cocaine in Lori Ann's face. "Call me if you need me."

Lori Ann went to work and got chewed out by her supervisor and her co-workers. "Three strikes and You're Out" was the last thing she remembered hearing. Lori Ann went to her car to smoke during her lunch break. She remembered she had a little marijuana in her glove compartment; she began to smoke it. The Company Security guard, who normally drove his car around the lot was walking. He caught Lori Ann by surprise. He told her to roll the window all the way down, so he could get her identification. She stepped out of the car and handed him her ID badge. "Ma'am, I'm going to have to report you for smoking an illegal substance on this property." Lori Ann offered him a hit and the guard pulled out his radio. "469 to Base – I have an employee smoking pot in Lot 216." Lori Ann leaned on her car continuing to smoke when the other guards came on the scene. They gave her a pink slip and a copy of the policy saying use of any illegal substances will be grounds for immediate dismissal. One of the guards asked Lori Ann, "Do you have any personal belongings that you would like to get before you leave?" "No, y'all can have all of that shit." Lori Ann yelled to the security guard who caught her, "you're a sellout." She was escorted off the premises while her co-workers watched from nearby windows and doorways.

"Where the wind takes me" Earl Klugh

Lori Ann did not look for work for a few months and when she tried, she found it exceedingly difficult. She began to hang out with other jobless folks in her neighborhood. She did not realize so many of her neighbors were out of work. Because she lived with her mother, the only major bill she had was her car note and car insurance. She would normally give her mother $100 when she got paid. Her mother would just add it to a big wad held by a rubber band in a shoe box under her bed. Lori Ann became less and less interested in finding a job and more interested in keeping a high so she could forget her troubles. She even stopped visiting Dennis so frequently. Lori Ann walked past the mirror in her room and didn't recognize herself. "Who is that?" she said loudly. "Who is that?" she said again. She fell on the bed, grabbed the remote, shrugged her shoulders and started flicking the remote to find something to watch. The television was watching her because she had fallen asleep.

Chapter 30

"In good times and bad times…" Dionne Warwick

Gail was driving home in between classes to take her mother to the grocery store. She had 2 hours and 35 minutes before her next class. Suddenly, she thought she saw Lori Ann walking aimlessly across the busy intersection. Gail followed her in her rearview mirror. She said aloud, "Is that Lori Ann?" She looked at the clock on her dashboard and realized she did not have a lot of time, but she turned the car around. She gently pulled up next to Lori Ann and rolled down her window. "Hey Lori Ann," Gail said in her best imitation of a happy voice. "Is that you Gail," Lori Ann said as she peered into the car. The light was gone from Lori Ann's eyes. In fact, she had deep dark circles around them. Her beautiful stylist clothes were now dull and dirty. Her shiny coal black hair was now matted to her head with gel. "Where are you going?" Gail asked. Lori Ann looked around several times as if she were being followed and said, "I'm going to the store to get some diapers. I had a baby three months ago." Gail tried to be happy for her by sitting up and smiling. "Did you have a boy or a girl?" "I had a girl and her name is Porsche Lorika; I always wanted a Porsche, remember?" Gail nodded, "Yes, I remember you trying to zoom in your car like it was a sports car, especially if we were going to the E Club. Lori Ann cracked a smile and began to walk away saying, "It was good seeing you Gail – you look really good." Gail followed her in her car for a few minutes wanting to talk more. "Do you want me to take you to the store? I was just about to pick up Momma and take her to the grocery store. She will be happy to see you." Lori Ann looked down at her clothes and looked inside Gail's car. "No, I have some other things to do." Lori Ann began to hurry off. Gail hesitantly began to roll up her window, "Good to see you; I can't wait to see the baby." Gail slowly drove off. She looked in her rearview mirror and wondered what happened to the confident girl she met 12 years ago. She continued to watch Lori Ann in her rearview as she turned the car around. Lori Ann was hailing cars; some cars slowed down, and she could hear Lori Ann saying all she needed was $5 or $10 to get her baby some diapers. She told the drivers she would be willing to do anything. "Hey, tell me what you want me to do, I'll do it – I just need $5 or $10." Tears began to well up in Gail's eyes.

They were both good girls and the best of friends. How did she let her friend become this person she did not even recognize? Gail loved school and Lori Ann tolerated it. Gail excelled in elementary, middle, and high school. She participated in all the extracurricular programs: softball, tennis, yearbook, cheerleading, newspaper, track, glee club, etc. Lori Ann liked to dress up and won *Best Dressed* for each year in high school. She was a below average student barely completing her exams to graduate. She had a few other friends, but Gail was her main close friend. Her other *friends* were using her to get clothes made, to get money for lunch or to get a ride home in her car. When Gail went to college, she tried to keep in touch with Lori Ann, but their relationship suffered because of their separate lives. Gail thought Lori Ann resented her for "leaving her."

Gail pulled up in her mother's driveway and she started down from the porch. "I was wondering what happened to you – is everything okay?" As Gail's mother got in the car and buckled her seatbelt, she looked at her daughter, "Are you Okay?" Gail put the car in reverse and said, "I saw Lori Ann walking down the street looking terrible. I stopped and talked to her for a few minutes. She told me she had a baby named Porsche. She said she was going to get the baby some diapers and I offered to take her, but she said no because she had some other stuff to do." Gail's mother leaned back getting comfortable in the car. "I heard she had a baby; I also heard she was on that stuff, too. It's so sad – what is this world coming to?" Gail chimed in, "I felt so bad for her; she was my best friend for the longest. I wanted to do something, but she rejected me." Her mother said, "You did the best thing you could do; you acknowledged her and offered some help. You cannot make people accept your help. It is sad that she turned out like that, but we will just pray for her and that baby. When she was with that drug dealer, what's his name, Dennis, she was okay and since he's locked up now, she has gone downhill like the others." "That's so ironic," said Gail. Her mother started to look through her purse. "Where did I put that grocery list?" Gail noticed the top of some folded notebook paper in her dress pocket. "Is that it?" as she pointed to her mother's pocket. They both smiled at each other. Gail turned up the radio when Michael Jackson's *Ben* came on the radio. She drove silently until they arrived at the grocery store. As she pulled into the parking lot, she could not help but think of her friend and all the times they confided in each other at sleepovers, summer walks and long drives. Tears began to stream down her face. "Gail, get that basket over there in case there aren't any up front," her mother ordered. Gail slowly walked towards the stray basket. "Pick up the pace, you know you have a class in an hour or so." Gail snapped out of it and fetched the basket quickly. "Will you buy me some vanilla ice cream and some plain potato chips?" she asked her mother in a baby-like manner. "I don't know how you can eat that together, but yes I will get it for my baby girl. Come on, let's hurry. I don't want you to be late for that *Social Work in the Black Community* class. I know you want to see what Dr. Snow is wearing today and most importantly hear his lecture today, right?" Gail told her mother that Dr. Snow, the head of the Social Work department was very handsome and very smart. He looked incredibly young and had a great relationship with all of the students on campus. He enjoyed talking to them and they looked to him for guidance. He played tennis after classes at the college courts; he had a nice physique. Gail did not really need the class for her major; it was an elective. She enjoyed the class and he was a great lecturer; she could listen to him all day. At the end of the semester, it didn't even matter that she made a C on the final exam. Of course, she did not dare tell her Mom she made a C. "Dr. Snow is the best; I try not to ever miss his class. We have time, it's okay." Gail smiled. She was wearing a new navy-blue sweater over a white tank top with her polka-dotted skirt and loafers. She thought the outfit screamed typical college girl and she hoped Dr. Snow would notice it. "Your preppy outfit is very cute," her mother said. "Thanks, I just threw something on today, because I knew I was going to be at school all day. You know we have step practice after my last class. Don't forget to pick me up at 6:00 in front of the gym. "Tell me again when I drop you off," her mother added as she crossed off items on her grocery list.

Chapter 31

"Got my own mind, I wanna make my own decisions..." Janet Jackson

"Here's the tricky part," Gail shouted as she taught the step for her other sorority sisters to learn. Twelve of them lined up in 2 rows of 6 in the mirrored aerobics room of the college gym. Gail had a natural talent for putting step routines together; she was the step captain. She was getting them ready for a Step Show on campus sponsored by the Student Government Association. "Come on ladies, let's take it from the top with the 1st formation. I don't want to be here all night." The ladies hemmed and hawed as they got into position. "5, 6, 7, 8." Gail leaned against the mirror in front of them and watched them closely as they did their first synchronized step. She yelled out, "keep it tight," every now and then if she noticed flailing arms or loose movements.

The grand prize for the Step Show was $1,000 and her chapter needed the money badly for an upcoming conference and they could use some of it to repaint their sitting area on Greek Row. They had a bench with a shield and pavement around it that looked faded from the weather – you could barely read their motto; *we strive to Serve Others with Love and Compassion.* It had not been touched up since last year. They also needed to buy more supplies for the students they tutored at the nearby elementary school. They provided incentives when the kids got good grades and good conduct on their report cards. They bought books, cassettes, t-shirts, tickets to sports events and movie passes. They provided refreshments at each session because the kids would grow restless from the long sessions. They would have drinks, snack cakes, chips, and fruit for them during breaks. They worked hard and the sorority sisters really enjoyed such a rewarding experience.

"Zeta Xi Zeta is the only way." They moved into a formation that resembled a soul train line – each sister came out and gave names of occupations. "Teacher, Writer, Doctor, Judge, Director, Lawyer, Mayor, Psychologist, Biologist, Social Worker, Dean, Librarian." Gail shouted out, "This is the last step, make it good." She started it slowly and the sisters joined in afterwards, making a new formation in the shape of a Z. Gail said, "Last time," and they stopped altogether with their arms stretched high. Renee shouted from the back row, "Exit time Sorors." She started a step and they joined in after the first round. They moved across the floor like soldiers in complete unison. "Keep going until you cross that last mirror," Gail said. "Don't stop the step until you are off the stage or out of the audience's view." When everybody had passed the last mirror, they collapsed on the floor with exhaustion. "Woo-hoo, Good job – I know the $1,000 prize will be ours. Next week, we will have a dress rehearsal to see how the uniforms move while we step. We do not want any mishaps or embarrassing moments. Crystal, who was leaning against a wall holding a cane for balance, nodded in agreement with Gail. She held up the cane and pointed to Gail like, listen to her, she is telling you the right thing. Her speech was a bit slurred and her walking was often off balance, but she could manage to get along well with little assistance. "She's right," she said. Everybody looked at her and smiled or laughed in agreement. She missed stepping but was happy to be hanging out with her sorority sisters again.

"Holding back the years, thinking of the fear I've had so long." Simply Red

Everybody gathered their things and started to head out. Gail, still using her Step Captain in charge voice asked, "Does everybody have a ride home? Most had a ride, was driving or had someone picking them up. They all walked out of the gym together, slowly dispersing to various parking lots. Renee, Gail, and Donna were the last ones waiting outside the gym. Renee's sister, Callie drove up, chatted with the girls for awhile and told Renee to come on so they could stop at the store. "Let's go, I got to get some detergent and go to the washer. I got two loads to do. Y'all be careful." She drove off with Renee leaning out the window still trying to talk.

"And then there were two," Donna said. Donna, a senior education major transferred from a junior college in Mississippi. She was very tall, very southern, and she had a thick accent. She was at least 6ft. tall. She had the complexion of a cup of cocoa with short curly brown hair. She had a shape to die for and she walked like she was a queen in a previous life. "Well, I'll be doing my student teaching next semester, so this will probably be my last stepping performance." Gail did not really talk to Donna much, so she felt awkward trying to make small talk with her. When Donna first arrived on campus a year ago, she wore her letters and all, but she did not acknowledge the sorority sisters until they approached her. Crystal and Renee were the ones who brought her to meetings and made sure she knew about the upcoming events, projects, and functions. It took Donna a semester to get the transfer credentials from her home chapter and now she is about to be inactive. She was not Gail's favorite person, but she loved her because she was her sorority sister. Donna slowly warmed up to all the sisters, but she still had a stand-offish demeanor. Everybody got used to her ways and accepted her wholeheartedly and unconditionally. Besides, she had a great head for business and she always had good ideas for fundraisers. She was the chapter treasurer and suggested opening a checking account, so their money was not floating around from person to person. She kept the books straight and her accounting system was outstanding. She always said, "Make money and the rest will follow."

Donna's boyfriend, Randy drove up. He played for the college baseball team and he was active in the Student Government Association. He was about as tall as Donna and they made a cute couple. He was always pleasant to everybody; he always talked as though he were campaigning or running for a position. He had a corny sense of humor that even though the jokes were weak, he always made you laugh. "Y'all ready for the Step Show," he asked as Donna headed around to the passenger side of his old truck. "We're getting there," Gail said. He added, "Well, you better put your pedal to the metal. I can't wait to see my baby step onto the stage." They gave each other a loving smooch. "See you next week," Donna said, as she stretched across Randy's body ever so gingerly. "Do you want us to wait with you?" Donna asked nicely. Randy looked at her lovingly because of that nice gesture. He put the car in *park*. "No thank you, I'm sure my Momma will be slowly coming around the corner in that canary yellow Chevette in a few minutes. Thanks, though," Gail said. "See you next week; be safe." Gail waved as they drove off.

The sun was starting to set, and Gail looked across campus; it looked completely desolate. On most Fridays, the campus clears after the last class of the day, which is 3:00. Here she was sitting on the gym steps at 5:30 across the street from a supposedly bad housing project. She began to wonder if any of the residents went to the college or dreamed of going to college. She started to notice children playing and cars driving by more frequently. She saw a yellow cab go by and she said to herself, "1, 2, 3 Good luck for me I see a yellow cab." She thought of Lori Ann and wondered what she was doing. When she catches the bus, she normally times it just right that she only has to wait five or ten minutes before the bus arrives. She never paid attention to her surroundings or noticed how large the housing project was before. It was just as large as the college campus. She began to try and size up the people in the individual units that she saw. She felt like Jimmy Stewart in Alfred Hitchcock's *Rear Window*. A car drove by slowly with three or four guys in it; they hollered out some obscenities that Gail simply ignored. "Hey baby." Gail did not answer. She's too good to speak to us, let's go get her." Gail pulled a book out of her book bag. She had three more chapters to read of Anne Moody's <u>Coming of Age in Mississippi</u>. She needed to complete it by Monday; she was sure her Literature professor, Dr. Gillis was going to give a pop quiz on it. If Dr. Gillis looked over her glasses and told you to make sure you completed an assignment, you could bet that there was a test coming. When the guys realized Gail was ignoring them, they sped off fussing and cussing. All she heard was "stuck up." She put her book away because it was getting too dark to read. She began to wonder if her mother was alright; she knew she would not forget to pick her up. She knew the gym was locked but she pondered the idea of going to the Student Center to use the phone. The Student Center was three buildings away and she didn't want to risk missing her mother while going across campus to call her. There was a store one block away, but she was not comfortable with the thought of going there either. She saw Tina, one of her sorority sisters driving towards her and wondered why she was coming back. She was driving her mother's green and black station wagon. They have had plenty of road trips in that wonderful Wanda wagon, as they affectionately called it. The car slowly pulled up and Gail walked up to the car, leaned in and said, "What did you leave?" Before she realized it was not Tina, she was pulled into the car quickly. "I got you now," a man said with a deep voice. He held her down like he just caught a fish or something. He grabbed her sweater from around her neck and used it to keep her face covered. Gail tried to squirm free. "Stay down and be still or I'll kill you; I have a gun right here." The man poked her with something that felt like the barrel of a gun. The metal was warm, and she could smell motor oil or cooking grease. Gail began to pray quietly. "Lord, please don't let this man hurt or kill me." She repeated it all the while he had the "gun" on her. After the mantra of prayers, Gail trusted that Jesus would not let anything happen to her after she asked Him to protect her. Gail began to plea for her life thinking she could talk her way out of this situation. "Please, Mister, my Mom is going to be real upset if I'm not there when she comes to pick me up. I left my book bag on the steps and I had 2 schoolbooks in there, not to mention her cassette player. I told her I would be waiting on the gym steps, so she's going to be frantic and go ballistic if I'm not there." "Just be quiet with your big words. I won't keep you long." The man's dry, deep voice had an unusual calm to it, and he didn't seem to be concerned about Gail's story. He continued to hold her sweater-covered head down firmly while he drove.

The ride was a bumpy one, almost like riding on a mini roller coaster. Gail rode quietly but began to feel like she had felt those bumps before. Gail remembered the bumps from when she was pledging Zeta two years ago. One late night, the big sisters blindfolded the twelve of them and took them to a cemetery that had a similar bumpy ride. They led them out of the car in different locations of the cemetery and they had to find each other by calling out Z. Once they found each other, they were able to remove their blindfolds. Gail only remembered seeing a historical landmark nearby and thought this is awfully disrespectful to be here. "We're here now," the man said with the voice that cut Gail like a knife against a chalkboard. "Pull your pants off so I can finish up, I've got things to do, but I will kill you and dump your body right here if you give me any trouble." He laughed with a snort. "Nobody will ever find you way out here; hurry up girl!" Gail slowly slid her pants down; she was terrified of the thought of this man raping her. She closed her eyes tightly and prayed for it to be over quickly. She heard a zipper and realized he was about to start. As he slid over from the driver's side to get on top of her, he opened her legs and attempted to enter. He did not have an erection and could not enter. He mumbled something about not being able to get it up ever since the accident. He kept putting his lifeless penis next to her vagina but there was no penetration. Gail sensed his frustration but dared not to speak. He kept at it for what seemed like forever. Finally, a brave Gail said, "My mother should be outside the gym by now, she's going to wonder where I am." "Be quiet," he shouted as he ran his hands up and down the shaft of his penis. Gail could feel the friction of his hands next to her thigh. She kept her eyes closed tightly while trying to avoid the oily, greasy smell of the man. She turned her head into the comfort of her sweater. She smelled the fresh scent of her lavender deodorant and a hint of body odor from her perspiration earlier during Step practice.

She started to think about her family, her friends, her sorority sisters, church, school, and fun outings. She slowly left her body and felt like she was ascending to the clouds. She wondered how her family would react to her untimely passing. She thought about all the support and sacrifices everybody made so she could go to college. She had flashbacks of her life in a collage of out-of-order memories: having birthday parties in the backyard, walking home from the swimming pool with her sisters, remembering her Grandma making her peanut butter sandwiches, feeding the hogs at her Aunt's country farm, receiving a medal at a National Honor Society program, drawing a hopscotch on the sidewalk, getting baptized at church, saying goodbye to her 7th grade teacher, running through the neighborhood with the track team, singing in the youth choir at church, waiting in the doctor's office with her mother, reading Archie comics, being an usher at church, meeting Lori Ann for the 1st time, eating raw salmon, sitting in the balcony of church eating candy, playing with her favorite Hi Dottie doll, watching her mother cook dinner, picking honeydew flowers and sucking the nectar, taking pictures at the zoo, riding the bus to college, playing jacks on the porch, enjoying an ice cream cone at the park, driving to the E Club with Lori Ann, swinging high before baling out, graduating from high school and on and on.

She did not notice that the man had eased off her and was zipping up his pants in disappointment. Tears began to stream down her face when she thought about her mother's reaction; she did not want her mother to have to endure such pain. She did not want to let her down. She dared to speak again. "My mother worked hard to get me in college and now you're going to take my dream away by killing me. Is that going to be satisfying to you knowing you stopped someone from being something – something great? Please mister, just let me go, I will not say anything to anybody. How can I? I have not seen you. Please mister!" "Shut up," he bellowed as he put the car in drive. He drove slowly out of the cemetery, making sure no one was watching him. "What color is your Momma's car?" he asked. "It's a yellow Chevette," Gail said excitedly. "I think I see her car on the corner down by the gym, but I'm going to drop you off on another corner. Do you understand that I'm watching you and I'll kill you if I hear anything about this?" Gail answered quietly, "yes."

The man stopped quickly and pushed her out of the car. As she fell out onto the pavement, she felt the buttons of her sweater hitting her on the legs. It was her favorite navy-blue sweater, but she wasn't going to turn back to grab it. She ran down the street smiling and crying. Her mother got out of the car after she noticed Gail running down the street. "Ma, what happened to you, I was waiting and waiting and then I thought I saw Tina, but it wasn't Tina, and this man put me into his car. He tried to…" Gail started crying uncontrollably. Her mother hugged her and lead her to the car. "Let's get out of here," she said as she closed the passenger door. Gail continued to cry and whimper all the way home. "Let's get you out of these clothes and into the tub," her mother said as she helped her out of the car and guided her into her bedroom. When she started to pull her pants down, Gail grabbed her hand. She collapsed in her mother's arms. "Lord, what happened to my baby. I'm going to call the police. "She rocked her back and forth for a while on the floor. Gail stood up, grabbed her fresh clothes, and headed to the bathroom. She took the rest of her clothes off, slowly got into the tub and proceeded to wash away the greasy, oily smell of that man. Knock, knock – Her mother knocked on the bathroom door. "Gail, the police are on the phone and want to write up a report. Do you remember the make and model of the car?" Gail knew the car was exactly like her sorority sister's car and could possibly call and get that information, but she said, "No, I don't know what kind of car it was." "Can you describe the man?" Her mother asked on the other side of the bathroom door. "No ma'am, he covered my head with my sweater and then he pushed me down onto the floor of the car. I couldn't see anything." Gail began to cry again. "Okay, baby, just relax. I'm just trying to finish up this call. The last question the police needed answering - *was there any penetration – did the man rape you?*" Gail sat up and sobbed for a while. "Gail, did you hear me?" Gail answered quietly, "No, he couldn't get it to do anything." "Okay, baby, call me when you get out so we can talk about it." She heard her Mom walk down the hall dragging the tangled telephone cord. "What do you mean you can't file a report?" Gail sank lower into the tub.

Chapter 32

"Glory days in the wink of a young girl's eye…"
Bruce Springsteen

This was Gail's last year at college and she was looking forward to graduating in May. December was a busy month and she was happy it was over. She promised her mother she would come home on New Year's Eve before all the celebrations and shootings started around town. She did not want her out and about with some crazy folks. *A bullet doesn't have eyes and it doesn't have a name on it and what goes up must come down.* "I'm so glad you're home safe and sound." Gail's mother was loading a gun at the coffee table. "I already heard from your brother and sisters. Everybody is home safe. At midnight, we are going to shoot off these rounds, pray and go to bed. I made some black-eyed peas and I'll fry some chicken tomorrow." "Sounds good to me," Gail said with a big smile on her face. "20 minutes before the new year – 1985." Gail bopped to the kitchen and got some wine glasses and sparkling water. "Momma, I know you don't like this water but take a sip for the toast at midnight, okay?" Gail waited on her mother's response. Her mother looked at the price on the bottle, "I don't know why you spend so much on this stuff; we do have water here." Gail added, "but it's sparkling." She looked at the clock, "10 minutes and we can say goodbye to 1984." Gail's mother continued to look at the bottle as if she was trying to figure out the funny name. "Pelligrinioli." She put the bottle down and continued to get the gun ready. One of her co-workers suggested she get a gun because of the late shifts she worked at the hospital. She never takes it inside the house or in the hospital; she keeps it in the car. For the last five years that she's had it, she has only used it for shooting at midnight. She shoots two times and then she lets Gail shoot two times. "Three minutes to go," Gail shouted from the kitchen. "I'm making some popcorn." She put enough shortening in a huge pot to cover the bottom, scooped up a cup of popcorn from a canister on top of the refrigerator and poured it into the pot. The stove was already on high as she put the top on the pot. Before she could shout one minute to go, her Mom yelled it from the living room. "Hurry up Gail, one minute before 1985." The popcorn acted as though it heeded her mother's orders and began popping. "I'm coming," Gail shouted. The popcorn began to pop out from under the top and Gail removed it from the heat. While she was looking for a big bowl, the popcorn continued to pop, and kernels were all over the stove and floor. She found their favorite popcorn bowl; it was white with blue and yellow flowers around it. "20 seconds," her Mom yelled. Gail picked up the popcorn off the floor and stove; she put it in the trash. She quickly emptied the pot into the bowl and hurried to the living room in time for the countdown. When she plopped down on the couch, Dick Clark was leading the countdown, 10, 9, 8, 7, 6, 5, 4, 3, 2, 1. They said in unison, "Happy New Year!" Gail poured the sparkling water and they raised their glasses. "Happy New Year Gail, I love you." "Happy New Year, Momma, I love you, too." They clicked their glasses and took one long sip. They put their glasses down and got ready to go outside and shoot the gun. Neighbors were already shooting and screaming in the streets. Gail grabbed the gun and said, "Let me go first, Momma." "No ma'am, Momma is first." Gail started waving the gun around like a crazy cowboy. "Stop playing and give it to me. Luckily, the safety is still on or otherwise you and your tomfoolery would have made it go off." Gail's mother took the gun outside, removed the safety, and pointed it upward and shot two times. She handed it to Gail who pointed it downward and shot two times. She shot again and the gun made a clicking sound as though it were empty. The phone rang and her Mom went inside to answer it. "Hey Aldwin, Happy New Year to you, too." Gail's mother watched from the couch while Gail pretended to be a cowgirl. She did some moves like on *Gunsmoke* when they draw their guns out of their holsters real fast. She started pointing it and pretending to shoot imaginary bad guys. "Okay, Gail, come on in the house," she yelled as she continued to talk on the phone to her son. "Yeah, she's outside acting crazy." Gail put the gun to her head and pulled the trigger; it clicked as though it were empty. Her mother beckoned for her to come inside. Gail aimed the gun towards the dirt and pulled the trigger. It shot loudly. Her mother threw the phone down, jumped off the couch and ran outside. She took the gun from Gail and put the safety on it. "Do you realize that could have been you – thank you Jesus!" She took Gail inside while she was still holding her close to her. Gail was in shock – what if she had pulled the trigger when the gun was placed near her head and it went off? She would be dead or in the emergency room. "Aldwin, Gail almost killed herself, I'll call you back. No, stay home, I'll call you back" Gail's Mom grabbed her baby girl close to her chest. "Let's pray. Lord, I just want to say thank you. Thank You – Thank you Jesus."

Chapter 33

"Baby tonight belongs to us – everything's right..."
Smokey Robinson

Gail was looking out of the window at all the corn fields and cotton fields as they traveled across Tennessee. She had finally graduated and was excited about her next adventure. While working on her senior project at the school library, she met a man. He wasn't a boy; he was a man. He acted like a man, he talked like a man and he smelled like a man. He talked about goals, hopes and the future. He did not talk about going to the next frat party or ordering new kicks. He was five years older than Gail. His name was Garrett Aiden McIntyre. He was tall but not lanky; he had a milk chocolate brown complexion with black-waved hair and dreamy brown eyes. He had nice skin, good looking hands, and perfectly manicured nails. "Looks like you're going to be here a while," he said to Gail as he noticed she had taken up the entire table with note cards, books, highlighters, journals, and yellow legal pads filled with notes. "Yes, if I want to graduate in a couple of months, I've got to make sure this project is close to perfect. I'll definitely be here for a while." Garrett seemed interested but did not want to interrupt her flow. "My name is Garrett and I'm completing my master's thesis, so I know how you feel – Happy Studying." He began to walk off as Gail whispered loudly, "My name is Gail and thanks." Gail smiled at the nice encounter and got back to her project. She could not help but think of Garrett and wonder why she had not seen him before. A few hours passed and she was tapped on her shoulder. It was Garrett. "Would you like to take a coffee break?" Gail looked up over her glasses; she looked at all her work and said, "Sure" without hesitation. "Let me gather up my stuff first," Gail said. "Okay, you can put it in my private study room upstairs," Garrett insisted. "That way you won't have to carry all of it across campus." Gail was happy to do that, and she felt even better when she saw it was a locked room. "This is really nice, is this just for graduate students?" "Yes, you're welcome to use it if you'd like. I'm defending my thesis in 3 weeks and will not need it the rest of t he semester because I'll be done! Okay, your things are safe and secure," Garrett said as he stacked them all neatly in a corner of the desk. "Let's go, we only have an hour and a half before the *Express Café* closes." Gail and Garrett walked across campus talking the entire time. Even though it was 9 o'clock at night, neither of them seemed to be bothered about the time. Gail talked about her home life, church life, sorority life and her undying friendship with her best friend, Lori Ann. She poured her heart out to Garrett about how she felt responsible for Lori Ann's drug addiction. Garrett tried to assure her that it was not her fault. Garrett told Gail he planned to be an engineer and that he would like to work in a big city like New York. Gail admired him for his big dreams. She loved the tone of his voice; it was noticeably confident and comforting. She could look and listen to him all night. When they arrived at the coffee shop, Garrett asked Gail to grab a table and he would get the coffee. Gail admitted that she was not really a big coffee drinker. "I know just what you'll like," Garrett insisted. "Okay, surprise me." Gail smiled as she walked towards the table. Gail sat down and realized she had never been in this coffee shop. She always hung out at the University Center. This place was brimming with intellects – smart-looking folks, probably all graduate students. They were all involved in what seemed like deep discussions. They talked with their hands and they were sitting on their legs or perched high in their seats to indicate the level of interest. "Here's a cup of hot chocolate with a swirl of whipped cream and chocolate shavings for you mademoiselle." Garrett placed the cup and napkin in front of Gail. She liked his style. She wanted to say, *no you're all the hot chocolate I need*, but she just said, "Mmmm, this looks good, thanks. What do you have?" Garrett answered, "coffee with a little hazelnut cream and a hint of brown sugar." He slid his cup across the table. "Taste it." Gail smelled it and said, "it smells delicious, but I'll stick to my hot chocolate; I don't want to mix flavors. "Did you want a cookie or some cake with it? They have all kinds of pastries up there." Garrett asked. "No, thank you, this is more than enough. I have some peanuts, sunflower seeds and cheese crackers in my bag at the library." Gail sipped her hot chocolate slowly without realizing she had a bit of the whipped cream on the top of her nose. "Now, you're hot chocolate with whipped cream," Garrett said, as he grabbed a napkin and wiped her nose. Gail smiled and almost melted when he touched her; he had a gentle touch and she longed for more. They were still talking endlessly when the lights began to blink off and on. "They're getting ready to close, so we should get going," Garrett said. "Okay, I enjoyed talking to you, but I've got tons of work to do." Gail began to get up and Garrett stood up and said, "I enjoyed it too – how much longer are you going to be at the library tonight?" "I'll probably be there until closing at midnight. I have a few more journals to cite and I must finish my annotated bibliography. I'm glad I parked close by the building." "I'll wait with you, so you want have to walk to the parking lot along." Gail breathed a sigh of relief. "Thank you, I appreciate that so much; more than you know." They headed back across campus. Garrett reached for Gail's hand and he did not let go until they got back to the library. "Do you want to work up here or back at your table," Garrett asked. "If I'm not in the way, I'd love to stay up here with you," Gail purred. Garrett pulled the chair out and said, "you're certainly welcome." Just as Gail was sitting down, Garrett leaned over and kissed her on her forehead, her nose and then her lips. "Let's get to it," Garrett said as he started flipping through the pages of his thesis. Gail pulled one of the journals and began to write the bibliographic information down on a note card.

> *"Have you ever loved somebody so much it makes you cry?" Brandy*

Garrett and Gail did everything together; they were like two peas in a pod. Garrett had defended his thesis and was set to graduate in May with Gail – he with his Master's degree in Engineering and her with a Bachelor's degree in English. Everybody knew they were a couple destined for happiness. *GG* as they were affectionately called had plans of moving to New Orleans and starting their careers. Gail was interested in pursuing her Master's degree. She sent away for all the college catalogs in the New Orleans metropolitan area. Gail loved planning and she was the queen of organization. While watching the barges go by on the Mississippi river, Gail began to fantasize on their lives together. Gail said, "Honey, give me a sheet of paper out of my green folder...and a pen." Garrett handed her a pad and pen. "Okay, let's talk about the trip and what we need. What if they hire you on the spot and want you to stay? What if they already have an office for you? What if they give you tickets to fly home and get your stuff? What if..." Garrett stopped her before she could say anything else. "Let's just wait and see what happened, "Garrett said. "I don't want to jinx my opportunity by talking about it so much." "You have the skills, experience and expertise, so it's a done deal. Be optimistic," Gail said. "Positive thinking is the mantra for today, so Yes, I'm going to get the job and we're going to move to New Orleans," he smiled. He picked Gail up and let her slide slowly down to meet his lips with a kiss.

"One more week before graduation," Gail's mother told the two as they sat at the kitchen table finishing up some peach cobbler. "Gail tells me you're going to New Orleans for a job interview." "Yes, ma'am and I'd like Gail to come with me. We can go to Bourbon Street when I finish the interview and do some sight-seeing." "It sounds like fun, huh, Momma?" "Yeah, I'm sure all the tourist attractions are waiting to take your money. Just make sure you bring my baby back safe and sound." Gail gave Garrett a big smile because she wanted her mother's approval. "Will y'all go somewhere else and play googly eyes; I've got to wash these dishes and get ready for work." "We'll wash the dishes," Gail volunteered happily. "Okay, that's my baby. Thank you because I am really tired today, but I've got a couple of more hours before I have to go in at 11:00p. I guess I'll go lay down for a minute. Y'all put some plastic wrap on that cobbler and put it in the refrigerator." "Yes, ma'am," they said. She walked slowly down the hall. Garrett watched her walk out of sight and said, "you're *my* baby – let's hurry up and wash these dishes so we can watch Johnny Carson's monologue." Gail gathered the dishes off the table and Garrett started the dish water.

Chapter 34

"...Now we're sharing the same dream..." Billy Ocean

"Sweetheart, do you need to stop for anything?" Garrett asked Gail. Gail was mesmerized by the sights along the highway. She felt free and calm. She had graduated, she had a wonderful man and they were on their way to New Orleans, one of the most beautiful places in the country. "No, I'm fine – thanks," she said. "I know you're fine baby, but do you need to stop?" Garrett asked. Gail loved it when he called her baby; it just rolled off his lips so perfectly. She loved being called sweetheart, but *baby* sounded so good. When Garrett said it, it seemed like he was declaring his love for her every time he said it. "No, I don't need to stop for anything – I'm good. Gail grabbed Garrett's hand and kissed it. She stroked his hair and face. She leaned over and gave him a kiss on the cheek, and he turned quickly to get a kiss on the lips. "I want some lip action," he said. Gail turned back towards the window and smiled with satisfaction. As she slowly nodded her head in contentment, Garrett realized she was off to sleep. He turned the radio to an easy listening smooth jazz station, checked the time and set the cruise control. He had 2 more hours of driving before reaching his destination. He looked over at Gail and began to stroke her arm until he reached her hand. Gail grabbed Garrett's hand and turned towards him so she could hold it all along the drive. She looked up and smiled and went back to sleep.

"We're here sleepy head," Garrett said as he grabbed Gail's thigh gently. Gail opened her eyes and noticed the beautiful trees lining the driveway leading up to the hotel entrance. "It's gorgeous; look at that entrance." Gail dug around in her purse looking for her disposable camera. "This company must really want you if they put you up in this nice hotel." She let the windows down and started taking pictures. The entrance to the hotel had lots of ornate detail around the doorway with ornamental metal sculptures strategically placed around the shrubbery. Garrett parked the car and grabbed his portfolio; it had his hotel reservation information in it. "I'll be right back, baby." He got out of the car and Gail said, "Wait a minute." As soon as he headed back towards the car, she snapped his picture. "Got cha." Garrett smiled and walked hurriedly towards the entrance.

Garrett came back to the car waving a key. "We're all set." He got in the car and gave Gail a big kiss. "I love you baby, let's put our stuff in the room and go sightseeing," he said. Gail was excited too, she knew that Garrett really wanted this position and the way the company was wooing him, they must have really wanted him too. "Okay, great - I can put on some sandals because my toes are dying for some air, Gail said while pointing and flexing her feet. "C'mon, because I want to make sure I've reviewed all the research I did on this company tonight," Garrett said as he opened the door for Gail. "I also want to review those cupcakes and especially that muffin." Gail smiled because she knew he was referring to her. "Okay, Mr. Engineer, let's go." As they walked through the hotel, it was like walking through a huge Mall. There were specialty shops, water fountains, small kiosks, and lovely artwork throughout the building. It had a nautical theme with sandcastles, seashells, etc. Gail snapped pics of everything. "Let's get a picture in front of this huge aquarium," Gail said. "Okay, but then let's go straight to the room," Garrett said. "Okay honey. Excuse me, would you mind taking a picture of us?" Gail asked an unassuming couple walking by. "Sure," the man said. "You must be newlyweds; where are you from?" Before they could answer, the lady was giving instructions on how to pose for the picture. "Put your arms around her and lean towards the aquarium," she said. They did as they were instructed and smiled. "Great, let's get one more shot just in case," the man said. They smiled again and the man said, "perfect, enjoy your honeymoon." Gail and Garrett walked towards the elevator smiling. "Okay, we're on the 6th floor." Once they realized no one else was getting on the elevator, they looked at each other lovingly and leaned in for a kiss. Garrett pulled Gail close to him for a long embrace. Gail pushed him away when she heard a chime from the elevator. Gail and Garrett separated to either side of the elevator once the doors opened; they looked at each other as though they had just got caught in the act. Two guys and a young boy walked into the elevator. The two guys looked up at the digital display for their floor. Gail and Garrett looked too and were happy to see that they were 1 floor away from their destination. As soon as the doors opened, they bolted out quickly, stopping only to see which hall led to their room. They ran down the hall like school kids on their way to recess.

When they got to the door, Garrett opened the door slowly. "You may enter now," he said in an official hotel staff tone. Gail responded, "I thank you kind sir." She plopped on the bed and began taking her tennis shoes and socks off. "This is a gorgeous room," she said as she wiggled her toes. She lay across the bed. "Honey, I can't move from this comfortable, plush bed, would you bring my bag so I can get my sandals out?" Garrett was in the bathroom, but he was not using it. "Okay, baby," he said. He came out with a tray; he had 2 glasses of sparkling cider and a plate of cheese, turkey, nuts, grapes, strawberries, and crackers. In the center of the tray was a black velvet box. "For you, Gail, I wanted to make this our special day. It seems like we have been together forever, so let's make it official. I cannot imagine being with anyone else but you. You are my sunshine and I want to be with you forever. I will try my best to make you happy." He grabbed the velvet box, opened it, pulled out a ring and knelt beside the bed. He took her hand and said, "Gail, will you marry me?" Gail began to cry. It was so romantic, and Garrett was so genuine and real. She loved him so much for being so thoughtful. She got on the floor with Garrett and said, "Yes, I'll marry you!" They kissed and embraced like a couple going off to war. "When did you have time to pick up all of this stuff? It is so nice – I love that you are so thoughtful, considerate, and romantic. Thanks for making me feel so special; everything looks so good." Garrett began to sing; *You Must be a Special Lady and a Very Exciting Girl.* Gail took a strawberry off the plate, bit half of it and put the other half in Garrett's mouth. While still chewing, they kissed; the phone rang. "You eat the rest of this," Garrett said as he passed the strawberry to Gail's mouth. He kissed her lips and went to answer the phone. "Hello. Yes, everything is fine. Please – that would be great, at 7:00 a.m. Thank you, Bye." Gail was nibbling on the snacks when Garrett turned and said, "I'd like to make a toast – to the most beautiful wife-to-be and the start of a great future." They clicked glasses and sipped their cider slowly. "I asked for a wakeup call at 7:00a since my interview is at 9:30; this will give me time to figure out traffic and everything. It's a backup in case my phone alarm doesn't work properly. Do you still want to go sightseeing?" Gail fed Garrett another strawberry. She popped a grape in her mouth. "Everything I want to see is right here." She looked at her ring and looked at Garrett. "It's the most beautiful ring I've ever seen – I love the 3 stones on each side leading to the diamond. Honey look at how it glistens in the light," she said as she grabbed his belt buckle and pulled him close. "I got some more lip action for you."

Chapter 35

"Take your burden to the Lord and leave them there." *Blind Boys of Alabama*

Lori Ann and her 6-year old daughter, Porsche were living in a shelter. It was nice; she had a bedroom with a connecting room for Porsche and a bathroom. She was trying to get back on track after being on the streets for the last three years. When Porsche was born, Lori Ann stayed with her mother for a little while, but Mrs. Keefer did not like all the traffic that was coming through her house. When things began to come up missing, she made Lori Ann move out, but she kept Porsche. Lori Ann began to come into the house while her mother was at work; she would change clothes, eat something, and steal small items that she thought her mother would not miss. When her mother came home, she would walk through the house missing lamps, vases, rugs, etc. She changed the locks and boarded up the windows after a television and radio came disappeared. Mrs. Keefer hated denying her child access to her house or to her child, but for her safety, she thought it was the best thing for Porsche and for Lori Ann.

Lori Ann was doing much better now that she had a stable environment for herself and Porsche. She had a part-time job at a warehouse and Porsche was in school. Her schedule was an easy one: take Porsche to school, go to work, pick up Porsche from school and report back to the shelter before 7:00 p.m. There were always fun things going on at the shelter for the kids and for the women. The shelter offered counseling and professional development workshops for the mothers. It was a safe place and Lori Ann loved it because Porsche loved it. If her daughter was happy, that was all that nattered to her. The kids had a library, recreation room and playground. The shelter encouraged them to do better and become independent. They could live there a maximum of five years. Once they found a full-time job and worked for at least six months, the shelter would pay 1st and last month's rent plus provide two rooms of furniture.

A few days before Halloween, Lori Ann noticed a flyer that said some sorority was coming to put on a Fall Festival for the residents at 6:00p.m. The flyer listed a scary lab, face painting, pumpkin bowling, musical chairs, costume contests and plenty of prizes. Lori Ann knew Porsche would love all those activities, so she wrote it down in her datebook so she would be back at the shelter in time for the fun. She looked at the datebook with sunflowers all over it. She attended a workshop on Time Management at the shelter a few months ago. At the end of the workshop, the presenter gave everybody a datebook and told them to use it for reminders and appointments. "This has really helped me stay organized and on time," she said to herself as she plopped it back into her handbag. As Lori Ann walked out unto the shelter patio to take a smoke break, she saw several folks walking by with the same dazed look she had on her face a year ago. "Lori Ann, I thought you quit smoking," said Pepper Dawson, one of the resident managers. "I'm really trying, Ms. Dee, but every now and then I have an urge, especially when I have some heavy thinking to do." "What's on your mind?" Lori Ann took a few more puffs and said, "They offered me a full-time job today at the warehouse, but what would I do about Porsche? They have aftercare at her school, but it is $20 a week and I would have to get there before six o'clock. I've checked the bus route and the bus would drop me off at 5:30 in front of the school. What if the bus is late? What if I miss the bus? They will charge $1 for every minute I'm late." Pepper Dawson looked at her and said, "You do have some heavy things to think about, don't you? On the one hand, it's great you'll have a full-time job, but on the other hand, you'll have to think about transportation and childcare – nothing any other mother doesn't think about when thinking about taking on a new job." They both smiled at each other. "I'll leave you to your thoughts; it will be okay." She walked off smiling and feeling confident that Lori Ann would make the right decision. "Thanks Ms. Dee," Lori Ann shouted as she took one last puff; she put the cigarette out on the back of her shoe and tossed it in her pocket. "I'll have this other half later – I really need to quit." She headed to the cafeteria to pick up Porsche.

The kids were finishing up dinner and taking their trays to the kitchen window. She spotted Porsche cleaning her area with a damp cloth. She walked towards her daughter and said, "Good job, baby, are you almost done?" Porsche gave her a big hug, grabbed her hand and said, "Mommy, come over here." She walked her over to a big sign about the Fall Festival hosted by the Zetas. Lori Ann looked more closely at the sign and noticed something familiar about the shield that she didn't notice on the smaller flyer in the hall. Porsche was tugging at Lori Ann's shirt for attention. Lori Ann wondered if these Zetas were the ones Gail was a part of while she was in college. "I'm sure Gail has graduated by now and moved on to bigger and better things," she thought aloud. "Huh, Momma, can we go?" Porsche said loudly. Lori Ann snapped out of her haze of thoughts and said, "Sure, baby, we can go. Let's go upstairs and get you ready for bed." Lori Ann glanced back at the sign and wondered about her friend, Gail. "She loved them Zetas," she said as she led Porsche out of the cafeteria. "What's Zeta, Momma?" "It's the group that is going to bring you a fun time next week – the Fall Festival! Lori Ann began to list all the activities as they went up each step. "Face painting, Musical Chairs, Costume Contests, Scary Lab, Coloring, Pumpkin Bowling and Much More. Porsche said "Woo-hoo" after each step. She was so excited; she talked about the Fall Festival the remainder of the night. When Porsche was finally down for the night, Lori Ann sat up in bed thinking about Gail and the fun times they shared when they were little girls. She also remembered their last encounter on the street and began to cry.

"Fun, fun, fun" Con Funk Shun

"We are so excited to be here to have some fun with the children again this year," Gail said to Ms. Emma Faulker, the Director of the shelter. "My sorority members and our youth groups have planned some great activities with lots of food and prizes." "Good thing many of the children start Fall break tomorrow because if it's anything like last year, they are going to be worn out from all the fun and games," said Ms. Faulkner as she led Gail down the hall to a huge recreation room. "You can set up everything in here." While pointing to a smaller room, she said, "this room is normally used for group studying, but you can use it for your scary lab." Gail plopped the box and bag down that she was carrying on the nearby table and said, "This is a perfect room; this will be great for our events. I know you are pleased with this new addition." "Oh yes, after that bad ice storm damaged the old building, I was happy when they decided not to try and renovate the old one but build a new one. It's bigger and better; the acoustics are better too. Noise doesn't bounce off the walls like in the old building. You remember how it would sound when you had your events in there?" Gail continued to look around at the new facility and said, "Yes ma'am, it was loud; I'll go and see if the others have arrived so we can start decorating and setting up. Is it okay to use tape on the walls?" "Sure," Ms. Faulkner said. "We always look forward to y'all coming; this is your 10th year isn't it?" Gail nodded yes. I'll go and get the volunteer forms for you to fill out and meet you back here."

Gail headed towards the main lobby to greet the other volunteers. Everybody was loaded down with boxes and bags. There were five parents who volunteered to stay, 21 members of the youth groups ranging in age from 7 to 17 and 9 sorority members. Gail did a quick head count, asked everybody to sign the attendance roster and directed them down the hall. "Are y'all ready to have some fun?" Everybody screamed, "Yeah!" Gail took her portfolio out of her sorority bag; it included a sheet for each activity area: face painting, pumpkin bowling, costume contest, coloring station, etc. Each sorority sister was in charge of a particular area. Gail called out their names along with the activity and pointed out where to set things up. She also let them know how many were needed for each area. The volunteers fell in where needed and the youth groups were distributed among all areas as well. Four of the older youth were charged with setting up the refreshments table. "We have 30 minutes before the children come in, so let's get to our stations and make sure we have everything together. Are there any questions?" Gail looked about and started pulling decorations out of a box. "I need 2 girls to hang this banner up and then drape the door with this door design." The banner read, "Zeta Xi Zeta – Fall Festival" with pumpkins and scarecrows around the border. The door design featured a cornucopia and a hay background. Two girls popped up and took the decorations like robots without speaking. Even though many of the activities were geared around Halloween, they did not want to call it a Halloween party because they did not want to offend anyone. Gail strategically tied black, orange, green and yellow balloons to chairs all over the recreation room. She was not sure how many would play musical chairs, so she asked her sorority sisters to set aside 15 chairs. Generally, there are 30 – 40 kids participating, but there are so many activities going on that they are all over the place. Sometimes the mothers hang around and play games also, so Gail makes sure she has some adult games like guessing games or trivia contests with adult prizes like make up bags, journals, perfume, and puzzle books.

Ms. Faulkner came in and said, "Wow, this place looks great. Here are the forms, please complete all the areas. Under the section for contribution, just estimate how much you think you paid for all of this. I know that a dollar store donated the toiletries and we will send them a thank-you letter." "We will too," Gail added. Gail completed each form and signed her name as the contact person. Ms. Faulkner grabbed the form quickly, reviewed it, and walked off saying, "Thanks so much, y'all have fun. See Pepper Dawson if you need any help." "I guess she was ready to go," Gail mumbled to herself. "Okay, back to decorations. We have 15 more minutes." A little girl asked, "Where should we put this jar filled with candy corn, Ms. Gail?" "Autumn, Go and ask Ms. Debbie where she wants to set up the guessing game," Gail answered. "Yes ma'am." Another girl came up and asked about where to put the extra Fall Festival activity flyers. "Just put them on the table outside of the door so they can see them when they come in –okie dokie?" The little girl repeated, "okie-dokie." Gail walked by each activity station and into the scary lab. Everything looked great and Gail had a few last touches to put on the tables. "Where is the box marked *table centerpieces*?" she asked aloud. "Here it is Ms. Gail," a little voice yelled from the back. Gail followed the voice and saw that it was one of their younger charges, 8-year old Christine, who spotted the bold print on the box. "Thank you precious," Gail said as she grabbed the box and headed to the front. "Do you want to be my little helper, Christine?" Christine ran towards Gail and said, "Yes ma'am." They began to place the decorations on the tables. Ms. Pepper Dawson came in and said, "Wow, y'all have really transformed this place; this looks great. Are you ready for the children?" "Almost," said Gail. "Just give us five more minutes." "Okay, said Pepper. I know you have been coming here for the last ten years, but I must remind you that you cannot take pictures unless the parents are with the children and they agree to it. Gail and others nodded as Pepper gave the instructions. "Let me take a group shot of everybody before the children come in." Donna helped put folks in place according to group, height, etc. "Say Helping Hands, Pepper said, quoting their motto: *Helping Hands to Improve Your Life*. I'll be back with the children in five minutes."

Gail gave Christine a high five as they put the last centerpiece on the table. "Everybody gather around please. Gail asked them to come out of the scary lab for a few minutes so they could have a brief talk and prayer." Gail asked everyone to join hands. "We have been coming here for 10 years but each year it's a different group, which is a good thing. This is a shelter for Moms and their children who have no homes for many different reasons. We are here to offer them some fun. I want you girls to realize how blessed you are and to appreciate what you have right now. Let's have some fun with them. Don't look at them funny; they go to school just like you, but this is the home they come to at the end of the day. These Moms are trying to do better so they can provide good homes for their children. This is a great first step. When you do not see them from last year, that means things got better and they are doing better. Let's give them a fun night they will never forget and remember to keep them in your prayers tonight. Gail asked Donna to offer a brief prayer." Donna came out of the crowd and asked, "Would you bow your heads, please? Lord, thank you for letting everybody get here safely. Thank you for all the donations we received to make this event a success. We come here to be a beacon of light for these residents tonight. Let the mothers have a few hours to enjoy themselves to take their minds off their problems or burdens. Lord, let the children forget for a few hours what they have been through and just have some fun. Lord, use us to make this evening a night they will never forget. All these things we ask in your son, Jesus' name, Amen." Everybody said, "Amen." "Thanks Ms. Donna – beautiful job," Gail said. Gail told everyone to get in place because they were ready to start. Everybody scurried off to their various areas and rooms.

Chapter 36

"We both are so excited 'cause we're reunited, hey, hey." Peaches & Herb

Ms. Pepper brought the children down the hall – they were walking quietly in line until they got a glimpse of their recreation room. They started pushing and screaming to be first inside. "Alright, they're not going to start anything without you," Pepper said, she tried to maintain some order as the kids rushed inside. The ladies of Zeta Xi Zeta lead them to a large seating area for the preliminary welcome, introductions and directions. On each seat was a treat bag, name badge on a lanyard, an empty bag and a list of all the activities. Members of the Zeta's older youth groups came around to each child and asked them their first name – they wrote their first name in bold colors on the white name badge. They placed it in the plastic holder and asked them to put the ID lanyard around their necks. Gail looked around and saw that the girls were just about done with the ID process. She approached the podium and tested the microphone by saying, 1902; this was the year Zeta Xi Zeta was founded. The microphone seemed to be working, so she invited all her sorority sisters on the stage by waving them up. "May I have your attention, please?" The children were still stirring about and now they were comparing lanyards, unwrapping candy from their treat bags, looking at their printed names and discussing which activity they would go to first.

Gail repeated, "May I have your attention please." Anxious for the events to start, the children turned around in their seats and gave Gail their attention. As Gail looked out at the audience of children, she did not recognize Porsche sitting on the second row. "We are the ladies of Zeta Xi Zeta Sorority, Inc. A sorority is a group of women in college and women who graduated from college. Can you see the letters on our shirt?" "Yes," the children said altogether. Pointing at her shirt, Gail said, "These are the letters of our sorority – say Zeta Xi Zeta." The children repeated it louder, "ZETA XI ZETA!" "Great, good job- we are here to have some fun with you tonight, but it's not just us. Let me introduce our youth group; they are called Future Zeta Xis because we want them to do well in school, go to college and join Zeta Xi Zeta. They are wearing sky blue t-shirts if you need any help. We also want to instill in them one of our main principles, Service. The girls are ages 7 – 17. These girls will be all over helping you and answering any questions. They will also be providing refreshments and playing with you. The games, food and prizes are all free thanks to the kindness and generosity of area businesses. Of course, you can also ask any lady in the orange t- shirt if you need anything because they are ladies of, pointing to her t-shirt. The kids yelled, "Zeta Xi Zeta!" "Okay," Gail said happily, look at your activity sheet and see what you want to do first. There is someone at each area to give you instructions. We'll take the little ones and everybody else, go have fun." The children ran quickly to the various areas screaming all the way. Within seconds, each area had lines of children waiting. There was also a line outside of the scary lab. Two Future Zeta Xi Zeta members stood their post outside of the lab: one with a bandana and one with a hand stamp. The bandana was to be used to blindfold each participant for the element of surprise and the stamp was used to make sure everybody had an opportunity to enter the lab at least once before allowing second or third trips. The child would be led into the lab by one of the Future Zeta Xi's and they would be allowed to experience various sounds, smells, and feelings. These props did not cost a lot: cold spaghetti felt like earthworms, wiggly Jell-O felt like body parts, partially cooked beans felt like eyeballs, marshmallows felt like skin, etc. They would touch these objects all the while hearing scary music, hearing screaming voices from out of nowhere and walking through spider webs.

Gail was chatting with Ms. Pepper as she was leaning on a wall when she noticed some of the mothers coming in to see all the excitement. "Can we play?" one mother asked. "Absolutely," Gail said as she walked towards the mother. "We have some popcorn, peanuts, hot dogs, candy apples and cotton candy if you want some good junk food. We also have some frozen slushy drinks in lots of fun flavors like the tuitty-fruity, bubblegum, watermelon and blue raspberry." "I want to play some games," one mother said. "Moms help yourselves! Here is a list of the activities and if you need any help, just look for the girls in sky blue t-shirts and the ladies in orange t-shirts." Gail began to walk off when she heard, "You're going to wear the dog and the puppy out of those jeans." Gail quickly turned around with a big smile on her face. "Lori Ann, is that you?" Lori Ann responded, "In the flesh." They hugged each other tightly. Tears began to roll down Gail's face as the memories of their childhood played like a slideshow in her head. "I've been missing my best friend - How are you doing?" Gail said. "The last time you saw me I was at my worst, but I've been here for the last 6 months and we're doing better than okay." Lori Ann looked around and said, "Porsche is in here somewhere." Gail beamed, "The last time I saw her she was a little bitty baby, how old is she now? Let's find her, "They walked arm in arm as they bopped from booth to booth looking for Porsche. "I see you found a friend," Donna said as they came upon her activity area. "Yes, this is Lori Ann, we were inseparable when we were 10, 11, 12, 13 & up; she's like a sister to me." Gail was radiant as she told stories of how Lori Ann rescued and schooled her many times while they were growing up. She talked about sitting in the balcony at church, talking about folks and eating candy while listening to the preacher. "Give 'em another hand," Gail said as she mimicked the pastor on how he acted when someone gave a speech or sang a song. "Pastor loved to give folks applause, especially the kids," Lori Ann said. A Future Zeta Xi Zeta came up and asked Donna about *pumpkin bowling,* so she said, "I hate to leave this walk down memory lane, but I'm needed elsewhere." "Okay, girl – go ahead," Gail said.

Lori Ann spotted Porsche and said, "There she is over near the cotton candy stand. She is the one with the cotton candy all over her face and hands." "She is too precious. We have some handy cleaning wipes over there, so I'll grab them and meet you over there so we can clean her up." Gail, still beaming, headed to the First-Aid supply table and grabbed the wipes. Lori Ann looked at Porsche sternly and said, "Porsche, you made a big mess; look at your clothes and *your* face is a sticky mess." Porsche had remnants of the pink cotton candy all over her face, on her shirt and on her pant legs. Before Porsche could respond, Gail walked up and said, "Hi Porsche, I'm your Auntie Gail; your Mom and I were best friends when we were growing up on Dunbar Street in North Memphis. We had fun sleepovers, we loved to dance in front of mirrors and we really loved going to parties." Porsche jumped in and said, "I'm 8 years old. My Mommy is 30 and we don't know where my Daddy is." Gail looked at Lori Ann and smiled. "8 years old – wow, you are so pretty, just like your Mommy. Are you having a good time?" Porsche nodded, "yes." "I'm going to the scary lab, *wanna* come with me Auntee?" Gail knelt to Porsche and said, "Of course I would." She grabbed the little girl's hand and asked Lori Ann, "Do you want to come with us to the scary lab." Lori Ann waved them off and said, "You two go ahead and I'll catch you afterwards; I'll probably be at the cotton candy stand." With a big smile on her face, Gail said, "I'll be right back Lori Ann, I'm going to the scary lab with my little niecey, Porsche."

Gail and Porsche walked towards the web-covered door that read, *Enter If You Dare.* Two *Future Zeta Xi Zeta* girls greeted them at the door. "Prepare *yourselves* to be scared," one girl said. "I'll need to blindfold you so please close your eyes and turn around," said the other girl. "Are you scared, Porsche?" Gail asked as she held her hand tightly while the little girl blindfolded her. "No, I like scary stuff," Porsche said as she bopped up and down with excitement. "Me too," Gail said. Both girls at the door said in an eerie monotone, "Enter the scary lab." Gail said, "Hold onto my hand Porsche, I'm right here." The scary music began to blast as they walked through spider webs and curtains. The *Future Zeta* girls guiding them through the lab looked at Gail and smiled asking for approval to do certain things. Gail nodded her head in approval and waved her hands like *do everything*. The Future Zeta Xi Zeta girls lead her to a table filled with bowls of creepy things. The first bowl was filled with cold spaghetti and they told Porsche to feel for the golden coin. "Little girl, you must find the coin in this well of worms." Porsche put her hand up and they placed it in the bowl. She cringed a little but dug through and found the coin. Feeling proud, she held it up high and smiled. One girl said in a creepy voice, "You have completed the 1st test by finding the coin in the well of worms, now you must do the 2nd one." She guided her to the 2nd long platter filled with jiggly concoction. "You must feel for the eye of newt in this vat of liver." Porsche lifted her hand up in the ready position. They placed her hand in the platter; she lifted it up quickly after the first contact with the cold wiggly jiggly concoction. The girl repeated, "You must feel for the eye of newt in the vat of liver. This is your 2nd test – only one more to go before the ultimate scare." Porsche reached up again, and they placed her hand in the jiggly concoction. She felt around, up and down until she located the glycerin ball. She held it up proudly. "Good job," Gail said. Porsche smiled and said, "What's next?" The girls chimed in, "The 3rd test is the endurance test – see how long you can endure a mouse crawling up and down your arms. Hold your arms straight out to your sides." Porsche held her arms straight down and Gail brought them up. "You got to hold them up high, sweetie." "Okay, I'm ready," Porsche said. The girls wound the mouse up quietly and placed it on Porsche's shoulders. It slowly crept down her arm and made it to her elbow when she flinched, and it fell off. "You have made it to the ultimate scare," they said. They lead her to another room where they removed her blind fold quickly. She saw flashing lights, mirrors and blood-stained bodies walking towards her. Before they could attack her, Jason, Freddy, and Michael popped up and said, *let us have her first*. She pulled Gail and they began to run. When they saw the *Exit* arrow, they ran faster towards it. They went through the curtains and ended up amid the festival. "Wow, that was fun, let's do it again," said Porsche. Gail looked at her and said, "I'm glad you liked it, but it was too scary for me. Besides, I must make sure the other children are having a good time and check on the different activities. I think I better find your Mom." Lori Ann walked up and asked, "How was it?" "It was really scary; let's do it together Mommy," Porsche said. "Let's do what together, you know I don't do scary Porsche." Porsche held her head down in dismay. Gail said, "We had a great time, it was really scary to me – I thought Porsche was going to want to leave, but she kept going. She's such a brave little girl." Porsche began to smile again. "Well, I've got to check on the other activities and get ready for the costume contest, so I'll see y'all a little later. You should go and get your fortunes read, *Shunda the Great* knows all and can tell your future with her crystal ball." Porsche gave Gail a big hug and waved goodbye. "I'll be back; I promise," Gail said sincerely. She looked up at Lori Ann and said, "Auntie Gail will be back." Lori Ann said, "Okay, we'll be here."

Chapter 37

"Whenever you call me, I'll be there..." The Spinners

Gail and Lori Ann were seeing each other almost every weekend. Gail was picking up Porsche, a now *Future Zeta Xi Zeta* and taking her to sorority-sponsored functions. She was taking her to community service events as well. Gail and Lori Ann shopped together. Even though Gail hated to shop, she liked watching Lori Ann shop. Lori Ann would pick up something with the intentions of buying it. She would hold onto it throughout the store and then when she got to the cash register, she would change her mind. "Let's go back to the store that had this skirt with a smaller pattern and elastic waist." "Which store would that be," Gail said. "We have only been to ten stores and you definitely do not need any clothes." Lori Ann would just laugh and say, "You know the one, stop playing." At the end of the day, Lori Ann would end up with the 1ˢᵗ skirt she picked up at the first store. Lori Ann liked loud colors like orange, fuchsia, yellow, and lime green. She could always find her size because she was a perfect size 6. Gail liked any shade of blue: royal, navy, teal, etc., and she loved polka dots - but she hated shopping. Most times she would pick up what she needed and be done. She did not like to eye-buy or browse. If she needed a blouse or a particular outfit, she would go in the store and get it – no comparison shopping and definitely no trying it on. She shopped at the mall closest to her. As long as there was a Dillard's, JC Penney, Macy's, or Sears, she was content with the selections. She knew the layout of each store and she could go in, get what she needed and get out.

"Let's go shopping in Southaven, MS; it's only 30 minutes away," Lori Ann asked. "Oh no, I'm done for the day. We have been out since 10:30 and now it is almost 3:00. Don't you need to pick up Porsche from your Momma's?" Lori Ann got in Gail's face and said, "C'mon, I heard they got a new Greek shop. I'm sure you could use another t-shirt or something." Gail sensing the sarcasm said, "You drive and let's go to the Greek shop first since you're trying to be so smart. I'm starving like Marvin – can we stop and get a quick bite since we have a long ride to Southaven?" Lori Ann smiled because she was getting her way. They headed towards the mail exit. "Okay, let's stop and get some Barbeque." While walking back to the parking lot from the mall, they realized they were in the wrong section. They started to separate but still in view while looking for the car. "I see it over her," Lori Ann yelled. "Okay," Gail yelled back as she headed her way. Gail met Lori at the car they put their bags in the trunk. "You're driving," Gail reminded Lori Ann. "No problem, but we are going to listen to some Sly and the Family Stone instead of Cyndi Lauper. We also need to get you some more jeans. I'm so tired of seeing them every weekend, pointing at them with quick pricks. I did not want to say it, but you are wearing the dog and the puppy out of them jeans. Gail looked at Lori Ann and smiled. "What?" Lori Ann asked. "Nothing, just drive." Lori Ann adjusted the seat to accommodate her long legs, adjusted the mirror, found the *Everyday People* tape, and popped it in the cassette player.

Chapter 38

"Right now I'm free, I've got the victory, I've got a testimony" Rev. Clay Evans and The AARC Mass Choir

Gail had been diagnosed with high blood pressure after her 1st child was born. Her doctor prescribed medication that she took every day. Garrett asked her every day if she was taking her medicine. Sometimes she took it religiously and some days she totally forgot. She was so busy with her job, her church, her family, and her sorority, that she barely had time to do anything, let alone take that one little pill. "Some people have to take 3 – 4 pills a day for their blood pressure," Garrett said. "All you have to do is take it at the same time every day and forget about it." "It's a time release pill, "Gail said, so I will be okay if I skip a day. You just keep taking your purple pill." "I will and I'm sleeping like a baby." Garrett said, folding his arms across his chest. "Sleeping more like a baby rhinoceros with all that snoring," Gail mumbled as she walked away. She blew him a kiss as he headed towards the bathroom. "I'm taking a shower and going to bed. Are you joining me any time soon?" Gail smiled and said, "You know it's too early for me to go to sleep – besides, I've got to make my lunch, iron my clothes, look at the mail, sign Junior's field trip form, write a few thank-you notes and review my notes for tomorrow's meeting." Garrett waved goodbye and puckered his lips for the kiss. "Wake me up when you come to bed." "Okay," Gail said. Gail liked the quiet house; she could catch up on her reading, recorded soaps, and her household chores. Garrett was a big help around the house, but he mainly made sure the lawn and landscaping was done. He loved working in the yard and there were several plants in the house that the maintained, as well. Gail did not have a green thumb, so she was glad Garrett did.

Gail walked around the house, looking at various things she could do; she looked on the living room coffee table – I need to go through those pictures and make a brag book for the in-laws. She kept walking towards her office. "I need to send thank-you's to the companies that donated items to my sorority event." She headed towards the family room. "I need to weed through these old magazines; I haven't read many of them. They're just piling up making a fire hazard in this corner." Gail looked through a few of them and then thought about how the kids are always needing old magazines for various school projects, so she left them. She headed towards the kitchen. "I still haven't hung up those copper molds and greenery I bought for the tops of the cabinets. I'll do it this weekend." She looked in the refrigerator and grabbed a cup of mandarin oranges. She reached in a storage drawer for a plastic spoon and began to open the fruit cup as she walked to the laundry room. She ate two spoonful's, put the cup down and began to empty the dryer. She carried the basket of clothes to the family room and sat it on a table, closest to the loveseat where she was going to sit. She turned the television on and proceeded to find her soaps. She was careful to make sure she was watching them in order; she was about 2 weeks behind. She hit play and said, "What is Erica up to now?" She remembered, she forgot her fruit cup and went back to the laundry room get it. Along the way, she spotted the mail on the hall table, so she grabbed it. Finally, she plopped on the loveseat and began to peruse the mail with *All My Children* in the background. "Jack, you've got to realize I've got to do it my way," Erica said in her most diva-licious way. Of course, she tossed her hair a couple of times and froze in a seductive pose as it faded out to a commercial. "Of course, you always do it your way, Erica," Gail said as she continued to sort through the mail. Garrett left the business affairs to her, so she paid all the bills and kept up with balances and outstanding payments. He trusted her to handle things because she was so organized and surprisingly, good with numbers. Gail sorted the mail according to priority and or payment needs. She rubber-banded the 3 piles and went to place them on her desk in her immediate action box. She would address them for sure, tomorrow. She sat back down and began to fold her clothes while All My Children was going. She had not folded three things when she began to feel nauseous. She got up to go to the garage where the juice and sodas were kept in another refrigerator. She sluggishly made her way to the refrigerator and tried to find a green can in the sea of red, orange, blue and black cans. Finally, she spotted them on the bottom shelf. She bent down to get the soda and almost fell from dizziness. "Whoa Gail, what's going on girl," she said to herself. "I don't normally drink from the can, but this is an emergency." She sat on the steps of the garage and drank the soda slowly. After about 15 minutes of sitting, she decided to try and get up. Still feeling nauseated and shaken, she headed to the bedroom to wake up Garrett. Before she could get there, she fell. Her head was spinning and there was a whistling sound in her ears. It sounded like a plane was about to land in her head." Lord, what is going on with me?" She began to sing, *"Take your burdens to the Lord and leave them there."* She continued to crawl to the bedroom; she tried to call out to Garrett, but the words would not come out. She crawled towards the bathroom. She felt like she had to use it, so she climbed up on the seat of the toilet. The only problem was that she forgot to pull her clothes off. She felt the moisture and began to realize what was going on. She always kept a nightgown on the back of the bathroom door, so she reached for it, but she fell in her first attempt. "Lord, help me," Gail pleaded. She reached again towards what seemed like it was miles away; she got it. She closed the bathroom door and proceeded to run the water in the bathtub. As she took off her clothes, she noticed how badly soiled they were;

she leaned over the tub and rinsed the things out. She slowly rose to hang them over the towel bar and quickly set back down to prevent herself from falling. She then noticed traces of excrement on the floor and side rails signaling her arduous route to the bathroom. She got a washcloth, some pine cleanser and began scrubbing the areas clean, all the while singing, "Take your burdens to the Lord and leave them there." From eye level, she looked as far as she could to make sure all signs of her struggle were gone. She got back to the bathtub and leaned over to rinse the washcloth. Finally, she took off all her clothes and got into the bathtub. She sat there while the water ran to fill. She had a pillow rest for her head, so she grabbed it and suctioned it to the wall of the tub. She leaned back and waited for the tub to fill. She drifted into a sleepy daze and when she awoke the water was at her chin. She immediately turned it off. The faucet was somewhat askew from the wall of the tub. It was slightly off center from what she remembered; Gail looked carefully but could not be sure in her state. She began to lather up and clean herself up. She had to let some of the water out to prevent a major spill. As she washed up, she realized what a miraculous ordeal she had been through and wondered if it was over. She slowly tried to stand up, listening closely for whistling or sirens. There was nothing immediately, but she sat back down to prevent a setback. She washed her hair and scrubbed her body tirelessly, trying to rid it of any impurities. As her senses started to come back stronger, she began to think about what could have brought this episode on so intensely. She knew she missed three days of her blood pressure medication, so she stood up and got out of the tub to get her medicine out of her the cabinet. She popped the pill in her mouth and got back in the tub. She cupped her hands and ran some water into them. She slurped the water up and sat back down to lean on the pillow. She sat there singing, "*When your body gets sick and you can't get well, God is a doctor, God never fails, He's waiting to bless you, With His outstretched hands, tell him your troubles, oh yes, He will understand.*" She heard Garrett's voice in her head, "You only have one pill to take. Some people take 3 – 4 pills for blood pressure." Gail pulled herself up out of the tub, slipped on the gown and walked slowly to the bed. She eased into bed trying not to wake Garrett, but he always seemed to know when she was there. Garrett mumbled, "I've been waiting on you, baby." Gail moved closer to him and whispered, "Just hold me." Garrett put his arms around her and stroked her face with his other hand. "Do you know how much I love you, baby?" Gail settled into his arms and felt relief, comfort, and love. "I know, honey. Thanks for loving me so much. Goodnight."

Gail woke up the next morning refreshed and renewed. She went straight to her Bible in her nightstand drawer and read Psalm 55:22 "Cast thy burden upon the Lord, and He shall sustain thee. He shall never suffer the righteous to be moved." Garrett was just coming out of the bathroom. "Good Morning, Baby, do you know what happened to the tub faucet?' Gail responded, "No, why?" "It appears to have been pulled from the wall or something." Gail said, "I dropped the shampoo bottle while I was washing my hair last night, maybe it hit the faucet." Garrett said, "It must have already been loose or something, but I'll fix it. He headed towards the utility room, just beyond the kitchen where his tools were stored. "Okay, Honey, my Handy Man," Gail said, smiling. "Hallelujah," she yelled as she closed the Bible. The kids ran past Daddy saying Good Morning as they entered the bedroom. "Are you ready for some breakfast," she heard Garrett ask. Everyone said "Yes." "Go brush your teeth and wash your faces and Mommy will make the biggest and best breakfast ever!" 3-year old Garrett, Jr. looked every bit just like his father and 6-year-old Rheanna was the spitting image of her mother. I'll go check on baby Rochelle. The kids scrambled to their bathroom. Rheanna helped her brother up on the step stool, rinsed his toothbrush and put toothpaste on his ScoobyDoo toothbrush. She then rinsed her toothbrush and put toothpaste on her Yellow Care Bear toothbrush. Garrett was waiting with his toothbrush up to his mouth. "Okay, Rheanna said. "Let's go up and down first. Garrett mimicked everything Rheanna did. She spat, he spat. She gargled, he gargled. She grabbed a plastic cup and filled it with water, he did it, too. She drank it all – he drank it all, too. She looked in the mirror, smiled and let out an Ahhh, while admiring different angles of her teeth. Garrett did it, too. Rheanna smiled and said, "Let's go to the kitchen my little copycat."

Gail was busy at the stove making pancakes. She had bacon and sausage cooking on the griddle pan. She beat four eggs in a bowl and added a little shredded cheddar cheese, salt and pepper. "Here are my little precious babies. Rheanna, please set the table and we will eat in just a few minutes. Garrett, you get the napkins and fold them the way I showed you. We need four napkins – one for Daddy, one for Mommy, one for Sister and one for you. Baby Rochelle has her own napkin – look at her sitting pretty in the highchair." Garrett walked into the kitchen with a wrench, "This should do it." "Breakfast is almost ready," Gail hummed as she flipped the last pancake. She put the platter of pancakes in the center of the table. Rheanna was just bringing the syrup to the table. Gail poured the eggs into a pan and begun to put the meats onto a serving platter. She carried it to the table. She called out to Garrett, as she finished scrambling the eggs. "Breakfast is ready – Garrett, go and tell Daddy that breakfast is ready." Garrett ran off since he had completed his napkin folding duty. "Breakfast is ready, Daddy, Garrett shouted continuously, as he ran towards the bedroom. Garrett came to the kitchen with Garrett under his arm like a football. "We washed our hands and we're ready for breakfast," said Garrett.

Chapter 39

"Here's my shoulder, you can lean on me." Kirk Franklin

Gail was at her mother's house with the children, when she did her usual looking out of the front door to see what was going on in the old neighborhood. She spotted Lori Ann, driving a beige Chrysler LeBaron convertible up to her old house across the street. Gail hollered to her mother in the kitchen that she sees Lori Ann and that she would be just out on the porch to try and get her attention. Her son Garrett was asleep in her old bedroom and Rheanna was in the kitchen with her mother. Rheanna loved her Grandma's scrambled eggs because she put "extra special love in them." Gail went out on the porch, with baby Rochelle, waved and called out, "Hey Lori Ann." Like old times, Lori Ann looked over and when she saw Gail, she ran across the street to her. "Hey Girl," she said. They hugged and Gail said, "what brings you to the old neighborhood?" "I'm just checking on my people, Lori Ann said. "Hey Baby Rochelle; she is sooo pretty, Lori Ann as she tried to pick her up. Rochelle immediately started to cry during the hand off. "You know she doesn't like anybody to hold her, except me, Garrett, Rheanna or her grandmother." "Yes, I remember from the last time, but she has to get used to me." "Are you having any more children? Lori Ann," Gail asked. Lori Ann quickly said, "I would not mind having one or two more. What about you, Gail?" Gail raised her hands in the air and said, "I've been changed - I've been fixed; I had my tubes tied." "Oh, that's good, because you seem to be mighty fertile," Lori Ann added with a smile. "You certainly don't look like a mother, but you're looking good in all this pink," said Lori Ann to Gail. "Why didn't y'all come to church - Where's my niecey, Porsche?" asked Gail. "She is at the house; I left her watching cartoons and eating cereal. She is really enjoying the Future Zeta Xi Zeta group. I had to buy her a calendar and a datebook to keep up with her meetings. Every week, she asked, "Mommy, do I have a meeting this weekend. We will be back at church, soon." Gail was wearing a pink drop-waist floral dress with pink pastel shoes. She also had on a pearl necklace with matching pearl stud earrings and a pink pastel headband. Lori Ann was wearing a black satin mid-riff top, a blue jean skirt and some black patent leather stiletto heels. Her hair was swooped up away from her face and it was shaved boy-cut style in the back and on the sides. She had about five holes in each ear, but only three had earrings of hoops and studs. Gail's mother came outside and looked at us both and said, "You girls are at it again, who are y'all talking about, now?" Because neither could answer, Mrs. Quincy grabbed Lori Ann and hugged her and whispered in her ear, "I'm sooo glad you're alright now." She grabbed her again tightly, "stay that way!" Teary-eyed, she quietly went back into the house to make the cornbread to go along with the dinner she prepared last night. They stood on the porch, which looked the same, complete with plants, like old times. Rheanna came outside holding a plastic fork with a paper plate of scrambled eggs and sat on the porch swing. Gail and Lori Ann leaned on each other, while looking up and down Dunbar street. Lori Ann said, "Can we sit with you, Rheanna?" They sat on either side of Rheanna and smiled at her and at smiled at each other. "Nothing can come between us; we have an unbreakable bond," Gail said. Lori Ann added, "Friends Forever - And don't you forget it." Suddenly a yellow cab drove by and they both hunched their shoulders and said, "1, 2, 3, Good luck for me."

Gail's Playlist

1 What Have You Done for Me Lately – Janet Jackson
1 When I Think of You – Janet Jackson
1 The Pleasure Principle – Janet Jackson
1 Nasty – Janet Jackson
2 Will It Go Round in Circles – Billy Preston
3 Just Me and You – Raphael Saadiq
3 Faithful – Raphael Saadiq
3 Missing You – Raphael Saadiq
4 Stuck in the Middle With You – Stealers Wheel
5 I Am Woman – Helen Reddy
6 Lovin' You – Minnie Ripperton
7 Head to Toe – Lisa Lisa & Cult Jam
8 That's the Way of the World – Earth Wind and Fire
9 Love Will Keep Us Together – Captain & Tennille
10 Pick up the Pieces – Average White Band
11 Jesus is on the Main Line – Lisa Knowles & Brown Singers
12 The Hustle – Van McCoy and the Soul City Symphony
13 Sweet Dreams – Eurythmics
14 Mickey – Toni Basil
15 Fame – Irene Cara
16 Luka – Suzanne Vega
17 If It Isn't Love – New Edition
18 Fast Car – Tracy Chapman
19 Girls Just Want to Have Fun – Cyndi Lauper

20 Yah Mo B There – James Ingram & Michael McDonald

21 Stuck on You – The Commodores

22 He Can Fix What is Broke – Mississippi Mass Choir

23 True – Spandau Ballet

24 Get Here – Oleta Adams

25 Let's Go Crazy – Prince

26 Hey Lover – L. L. Cool J

27 Caught Up in the Rapture – Anita Baker

27 Let's Stay Together – Al Green

28 Run to You - Whitney Houston

29 Time in a Bottle – Jim Croce

29 Where the Wind Takes Me – Earl Klugh

30 That's What Friends Are For – Dionne Warwick

31 Control – Janet Jackson

31 Holding Back the Years – Simply Red

32 Glory Days – Bruce Springsteen

33 Cruisin' – Smokey Robinson

33 Have You Ever – Brandy

34 Caribbean Queen – Billy Ocean

35 Fun, Fun, Fun – Con Funk Shun

35 Take Your Burdens to the Lord and Leave it There – Blind Boys of Alabama

36 Reunited – Peaches & Herb

37 I'll Be Around – The Spinners

38 I've Got a Testimony – Rev. Clay Evans and The AARC Mass Choir

39 Lean on Me – Kirk Franklin